MUST LOVE DRAGONS

A FATED MATES DRAGON SHIFTER ROMANCE

MICHELLE ZIEGLER

Hearth Publishing

INTRODUCTION

He doesn't know what kind of witch he's dealing with.

Kal had no idea what he was walking into when he met Maddie. She might believe that men aren't from Mars, but he sure isn't from Earth.

Maddie has enough crazy in her life with one ghost too many haunting her. Too bad fate just threw her a man claiming to be a dragon shifter. If Maddie chooses to accept Kal isn't crazy, she might be in for the ride of her life. Of course, if she chooses to believe him she'll have to leave her old life behind.

Kal needs to find his mate before his dragon's magic consumes him. He might have infinite cosmic powers, but he also has a soul that can't control the power of the universe. Not without Her. Maddie might be the right witch for him, except the fact she just cursed him to be a chicken. What the hell kind of planet is this anyway?

Publisher's Note: This is a work of fiction. Names, character, places, and
incidents are a product of the author's imagination. Locales and public names
are sometimes used for atmospheric purposes. Any resemblance to actual
people, living, or dead, or to businesses, companies, events, institutions, or
locales is completely coincidental.

To my daughter, who will someday be able to read my books. Your imagination is an inspiration.

ACKNOWLEDGMENTS

There's a lot to go into each and every book. My family always comes first, but they also support me and this crazy 'job.' I married my hero. The man who supports my dreams.

I have so many readers to thank, but especially my Beta/Alpha readers. Thanks Lucia, Heather, and Donnie! They have a knack for reading between the lines. Beverly, Shannon, and Carol Z. you are amazing support and awesome cheerleaders.

Of course, my review team is a group that has my undying gratitude!

Lastly - thank you readers! Thank you for giving me a chance and escaping into my world!

*M*addie squinted as her eyes adjusted to the darkness of the bar.

Blink. Blink. Blink.

A blast of air conditioning sweet relief on her burning skin. The sun baked Roswell like it was the egg on a sidewalk. Home of the creepy and unexplained. God, she'd left this town years ago and now she was back.

"Well, look what the cat dragged in."

Rolling her eyes, she gave a half-smile to the bartender. "Ellen, nice to see you too."

"Maddie, get your ass over here. You know I'm just joshing you. But really. You look like you've had a rough day. What has you coming back to our little neck of the desert?"

Blowing out a breath, Maddie strolled towards the wooden counter with dents and dings marking its adventures over the years. She chuckled. *This bar is like my spirit animal.*

Enough of comparing herself to a slab of weathered wood. "Same old, same old. My mother called me and basically wouldn't talk to me until I came back. Only thing is, she hasn't exactly shown herself yet."

Ellen smiled. "Your mother always was an odd one, wasn't she? I'm sure she'll be back around soon. How long are you planning to stay?"

Maddie ran a hand over the barstool and when it came back only marginally sticky, she sat.

"Hard to say. You know my mother. Always has something up her sleeve."

Ellen nodded as she wiped down a glass. "Yeah. She was always good at throwing the poor town for a loop. One too many futures and cheating spouses. Poor woman. Hey, have you seen the house -"

"Ellen. Another," said someone across the room. Maddie didn't bother looking. This town always had new people, mostly paranormal beings, maybe something unexplainable, aliens she supposed, and sometimes an oddball human here and there.

Maddie tried to think back to the last conversation she'd had with her mom. Marriage, settling down, and stability all came to mind. Maddie didn't like stability. She loved traveling, loved her work. Or she had. Right up until her show was canceled. How in the hell did a real ghost hunter show get canceled?

The network said she wasn't authentic enough for the audience. Maddie flicked her finger and a shot glass appeared.

"Maddie. You know we have glasses here. But, sure. This one's on the house."

Ellen plunked down another shot and poured the tequila. "One for old times." Ellen nudged the glass with her finger. "Bottoms up."

Maddie followed and nearly gagged on the burn, coughing as she dragged in air past the searing sting of the alcohol.

"Been a while then?" asked Ellen.

Sucking in a breath, Maddie nodded and wheezed a response against her windpipe's desperate plea.

"Yes," was all she croaked out.

Ellen laughed. "Definitely not the old Maddie I remember. You put us all to shame back in the day."

Yeah, she put everyone to shame because she'd constantly tried to drown out her mother's predictions.

Maddie finally got a breath in, her eyes stopped watering, and her words found their way out.

"Yeah. I don't really drink anymore, or well, I hadn't until now."

Flashes down memory lane raced through her brain like the Indy 500. This place was full of memories. Ones that she'd rather forget. Maddie wanted to know why her mother stayed, but it was obvious. The magic, that was why. Even in her death, her mother could still see the future. This town had so much magic flowing through its veins it gave her more power. Towns all over the world intersecting power spots, ley-lines, whatever. Roswell was one, and it hid in plain sight.

All that magic though and yet her mother didn't see and stop her own death.

"Yeah. No. Not the old Maddie."

Ellen smiled. "It's okay. Just glad to have you back. You're in time for the grand opening of a new club. It's owned by some Fae, and as creepy as they are; they know how to party."

She stiffened. "Locals?"

Ellen shrugged. "No. I don't think so. Guess I didn't ask around enough." She smiled. "But, let's not let that stop us. Be right back."

Ellen hurried down the bar to someone else Maddie didn't recognize.

Maddie scanned the room. Not much ever changed in Roswell, except that somehow it always did.

She rolled the empty shot glass between her index finger and thumb, listening to the scrape of glass against the wood. Why in the hell had she come back? Nothing good ever came from this town, not for her. Oh, right. She came back because her mother refused to talk to her until she did. That woman's soul needed to rest already, but no. Instead, she stayed here until she wanted something, and then made Maddie go crazy until she came back.

The door opened, spilling in daylight. Shielding her eyes with a hand, two large figures eclipsed the bright white of the outside.

Rolling her eyes, she went back to glaring at the glass. She needed another drink. Her mother would find her at some point, might as well just stay put. She had nowhere else to go anyway.

The thud of heavy boots thunked against the wood-plank floor. This bar was a dive, always had been, and apparently always would be. She didn't need to look up to know the original bullet holes were still in the mirror. Always would be. You didn't forget some showdown from the turn of the century. No. This town never forgot a thing. And now, she'd never forget the crappy wooden floor either. More clunking. *Good Lord! Sit down already.*

She scratched at her forearms, her skin itching and her magic jumping up like hell's flames were out to burn her alive. Sniffing the air, she swore it smelled like a mix of cinnamon and sweat. Glancing at Ellen, Maddie would need to ask what drink she'd made.

As the heavy boot steps grew closer, her magic started to do a conga line along her nerves.

"Son of a bitch." She scratched her thighs, rubbed the palm of her hands over her upper arms, shivering as the annoying dance stopped at the sound of a male voice.

"Are you okay?"

A zap of magic shot through Maddie and her libido decided now was a good time to wake up. Pressing her legs together, anything to stop the warmth growing within her. The stranger's voice waking places that she'd sworn were dormant, probably dead.

Slowly, Maddie turned her head expecting to be eye-to-eye or maybe eye-to-throat to a man. Instead, her gaze traveled up and up. Stopping at the most amazing orange-gold eyes.

What kind of creature was he?

"Wow."

His tongue ran over his bottom lip as he turned a smile on her. Maybe that scorched the panties off of every woman within a two-mile radius, but no way would it work with her.

"I'm not in the mood," she said.

Maddie squeezed her legs tighter, her body screaming she was definantley in the mood.

She closed her eyes. No. She didn't want him.

No, she wanted him, but she wasn't in the mood for a one-night stand. His muscles screamed that he got what he wanted every time and left a trail of broken hearts behind him.

Maddie tried to look away as her eyes flicked to the bulge in his pants. Son of. What was wrong with her.

Nothing was wrong with her. She was a female, he was a male and she couldn't remember the last time she'd had the weight of a man on her.

Maddie just needed to breathe.

Breathe.

"Want to come back to my ship?"

Pausing her thoughts, she glared at him. His voice smooth like a river of melted caramel, but his words were like the skipping of a needle over vinyl.

"Excuse me?"

He grinned, and well damn, she liked it. She liked the way the heat swirled within her, reminding her that she was alive. But no. No way.

"Want to come back to my ship?"

"Oh, you did say that. Well, damn it. All looks and no brains. Wonderful. Dream shattered. Is that seriously your pickup line? It's the worst pickup line I have ever heard. This is a desert … you know that right? No ship needed."

"A what line?"

Damn. His voice was toe-curling sexy. Or maybe it was the freaking bulge in his jeans she continuously struggled to ignore.

No. Just no. snap out of it.

"A pickup line. A line used to get some dense female to engage with you," Maddie said.

The man tilted his head and crossed his arms over his chest.

Her jaw dropped. He was huge. Even his forearms were corded in muscles.

"I'm not sure what you're talking about. Density has nothing to do with my interest. I was asking if you would like to come home with me. Which, right now, is a spaceship."

Damn. He was one of those Area 51 nuts.

"Yeah. That's probably not a great idea," Maddie said.

Maddie noticed the second mountainous man as he whispered something to her own wet dream. Her orange-eyed beast nodded and turned that heated gaze back on her.

"Perhaps I should restart? My name is Kal. This is my brother, Eadric. Do you have a name?"

She had to stop and run every retort through the mental filter in her head. Why did she attract the strange ones? The ones who didn't get the 'go the hell away' sign flashing across her face.

Maddie swallowed her answer, but her magic jumped and writhed against her skin as he took a step closer.

What the hell?

She needed to ignore him, but her magic refused. The more she fought him, it, whatever it was, the worse the itch grew.

This sucks. She scratched again. The static tickle wasn't going away. Looking up, his orange eyes never faltered from her.

Creepy, if he wasn't so damn hot.

Right. Name. Give him her name and maybe he'd leave. Wait, no. No. He didn't need her name. That's how you got murdered. Or, was that something else? Who cared. She wouldn't engage in this.

"You're not from around here obviously." She shook her head. "No. No. I don't have a name. My mother refused to label me as a young child. She just yelled girl for years."

The guy nodded. "We can give you a name, then. Something from my people, if that suits you." He turned to his friend and shrugged.

Maddie opened her mouth and then shut it. She closed her eyes and then opened them. "I'm not sure that we're communicating right now. I'm telling you that I'm not interested in whatever it is you're selling. But thanks. Have a great night."

Pulling away from the bar, she turned the stool and started to remove herself from its less-than-clean surface. Maddie stopped as his hand rested against her forearm, the heat surging from an invisible pulse between their contact.

Gritting her teeth she spoke. "Get your oversized hand off of me." Fear wasn't winning though. She wanted him. God. Why? Why did her body wake up for this wack-job?

Maddie channeled her anger because right now her damn body betrayed her.

"Remove your hand. I don't care what you are, you do not have the right to just claim any woman you want. You can't go about touching anyone you want. I will give you one chance since I know that not all shifters are civilized."

His hand didn't move. "I don't understand. What is a shifter? A person who shifts into what?"

Maddie rolled her eyes. "I can tell by your eyes. You turn into some kind of animal."

He nodded. "I turn into a dragon. Is that what you call a shifter?"

God. This guy. Dragon? Really? She'd never heard that one before. He was already walking sex. She swallowed. Not that Maddie had noticed the walking sex part. Nope. She didn't need his kind. She didn't need his trouble.

Dragon, that wasn't real. Was it? His hand was huge, maybe he called his man bits a dragon. Even creepier. Dragon though. Maddie rolled her eyes. Right. If he didn't want to tell her, then fine.

"Fine. You don't have to tell me what you really are." Maddie snapped her fingers and a shot appeared in her hand. Drinking, drinking was the answer.

"Maddie. This is a bar. Please don't make your own

drinks," said Ellen as she passed back down to the end of the bar.

Maddie tossed it back. "Sorry. Long day. I'll pay for it, I..."

Maddie flashed a glance at Ellen hoping she'd get rid of this guy. She couldn't stop herself from coming right back to him. Man, he was good looking.

Down girl.

"Maddie, is it?"

"Gee, thanks, Ellen," she mumbled.

So much for women having each other's backs.

"If I tell you yes, will you go away?"

"Maddie? Please understand my intentions. I've come here for you. I've traveled lightyears to find you. You, Maddie, are the most beautiful woman I've ever seen. I don't have much time, but if you let me, I'll spend the rest of eternity showing you that we are made for each other. That you are mine."

Wide-eyed, Maddie ran over what he'd just said. Worst or best pickup line? And eternity? His? No. That was not going to happen.

"Aw. So cute. Did you follow her down here? Maddie, you didn't mention you had such a sexy man. No wonder you dumped -"

Maddie glared, cutting her off. "Yeah. No. Thanks though. I don't need any crazy stalkers. I'm sure if you wait long enough though, you'll find someone desperate." She turned to Ellen next. "He is not my anything. I just met him. Don't you have a bouncer or something?"

Ellen looked from Maddie to Kal.

"Yeah. He seems fine to me. Besides, the bouncer doesn't work this early."

The guy, Eadric she supposed, moved. Oh, right. There

was someone else here. Damn it. How in the hell was she so blinded by crazy dragon shifter dude?

"Maddie. You're my mate. I am yours." He stepped closer and she couldn't move. Her brain said to, but her magic reached for him. "My brothers and I have come a long way to find you. I have come a long way to find you. I do not need, nor do I want anyone else."

He leaned closer to her. His hand slipped down her arm.

A slow burn slithered out where he touched her, it didn't hurt though. The heat traveled up her arm, blossoming as it spread into her chest. A power she'd never felt before surged through her. What is he?

What was she supposed to say to him? He wasn't being honest and now he just assumed she would want him? Lord, he just needed to stop.

She sucked in air.

Oh-my-God. She'd forgotten how to breathe.

No. Maybe. He needed to go. No one was meant for her.

"That's it. I'm done. Thanks for playing," said Maddie.

With a snap of her fingers, Maddie watched as he folded and shrunk. A snort escaped her lips as feathers sprouted out of his once handsome face and his orange beak began squawking.

"By the goddess. What have you done to my brother?" said the other guy.

She snorted. "I got him to stop asking me stupid questions. Now, do I have to explain to you that I won't be seeing anyone's 'ship'." She air quoted the word.

At least she could breathe, now that he was flapping his little wings. It wouldn't last for too long, just long enough to get rid of these two.

"Maybe he'll act a little more civilized next time. Here-"

The guy's backside was all she saw as he ran out the door.

"Wait! Take your - well shit."

She glared down at the chicken pecking the floor.

This was backfiring. What the hell was she supposed to do with a damn chicken? Well, man. He obviously wasn't a chicken and wouldn't be for long. Maybe, at least he would be a little more humble when he turned back.

Blowing a hair out of her face, Maddie had to admit she enjoyed his human form much better than a chicken. What the crap.

She didn't have time for a chicken, let alone a man.

"Maddie! What did you do? You know better. You're not supposed to transfigure anyone in my bar. Besides, I think chickens violate health codes."

Letting her head fall back, she glared at the ceiling. "Mom? Where the hell are you?"

Time to go find her, right after she fixed Mr. Space-ship.

2

*K*al's head throbbed. Had he just lost a fight? He never lost a fight. What had he been fighting? Something big? Had to have been. No, wait. Not a fight. A bar.

He'd been known to hit up a bar or two in the colonies back home. Kal shifted, his body struggling to remain perched on whatever it was he laid on. Something soft, that was good. His head swam.

"Eadric?" The sound, hoarse and far too quiet, scratched against his parched throat. Good goddess. Was that his voice? What had they done to him?

He tried to pry his eyes open, but the light burned. His dragon grumbled, his soul just as clueless.

"Eadric? Where are we? God. Worst dream ever. I was hunting an eisech and was ready to pounce. I went for it and that's when I saw them. My fucking claws, gone. Fuck, man. I had these tiny little feet, like a bird. And my arms flapped around, but I couldn't get off the ground. I damn near shit myself."

Someone laughed and Kal's eyes flew open at the unfamiliar female sound.

"Thank you for that laugh. What was your name again? Kal? Oh, my God. I haven't laughed that hard in a while."

"What in the goddess's name." He jolted up, the shriek of wooden legs protesting against the floor.

"You - you stay away from me you, you -"

She smiled. "I'm a witch. And I wouldn't have turned you into a chicken if you would have respected the fact that I said I wasn't interested."

"I don't understand." He shook his head and instantly regretted it. He reached back a hand, trying to ground himself. Looking for anything that wasn't swimming with the rest of the room.

The female came towards him, and he backpedalled, hitting something hard.

Kal wasn't helpless, and he sure as shit didn't like that she had made him feel that way. Some mate. What had the goddess done? How did he end up with this - this horrid female?

Oh, goddess. His hand flew to his head. Whatever he'd eaten for lunch might stage a reappearance if the damn room didn't stop its orbit.

"Oh, just stop being a baby. Come here."

He shivered as her hands rested against his forearm. Kal tried to focus on her touch, a warmth running through him rivaling his own fire. His tattoos glowed a bright orange and heated where her fingers rested.

As the room slowed, he focused on the creature before him. Kal couldn't look away from her mouth. Her lips formed words he didn't bother to understand, and damn, did they look sexy doing it.

13

The cloud in his head cleared, leaving his body ready to recognize what was happening.

Kal still questioned what he'd done to deserve this witch's wrath. His dragon's instinct had led him here, to this woman, the woman fate had chosen. She'd made his already hot blood rise to a boil. His mouth watered at her scent, and yet, she'd just turned him into a -a - what the hell was it? A chicken?

And then, the next thing he knew he was running for his life.

"I don't understand what you find funny, m'lady."

Her lips twitched at the corner and her nose wrinkled. "M'lady?"

Maddie shook her head once. "Whatever. I didn't expect you to run away when I turned you into a chicken. I'm sorry that you got chased by a lizard. In your defense, he was really big."

Kal blinked slowly. "A what? Wait. I don't care. Why am I in here? If you don't want me, why am I here?"

How could she not want him? Even after this trick, he'd still take her to bed. Hell, who needed a bed?

Kal watched her. He tried to tap into her thoughts, something he should be able to do with his future mate. Back home everyone with the blood of the Ammit people could speak telepathically. Maybe he was wrong. Maybe she wasn't his mate? Or maybe nothing was what it seemed here on Earth. Magic he'd never seen before flowed through this woman's veins.

"My commander had said you were a simple people. If you are, then how did you turn me into, what was it? A chicken?"

She glared at him.

"You are so strange. Should we just start from the beginning. I'm a witch. I have magic, and when I don't like someone I just do things. So, then I brought you to the back office. Of the bar. All because your brother wouldn't take you and I was told a chicken violated the health code. This backfired. Lesson learned, again. Don't transform people."

Memories of being small, tiny, and flightless ran through him. He shuddered. Fear and disgust, both things he'd never felt before, surfaced.

This would not do. His mate was supposed to want him. Worship him. Sniffing the air, she scented of a strong magic.

"You're not just a witch, are you, Maddie?"

Removing her hands, she stood back, and crossed her arms over her chest.

His dragon lost its shit and roared within his soul. He wanted to grab her and spank her for what she'd done. He wanted to grab her and mark her right here. Maybe the dragon knew what he was doing.

Nothing made sense. She should want him, beg for him. Instead, he was the one adjusting his stance as the need for her sank in. Kal felt helpless. Not good. He'd never been turned down before. He was a warrior, an elite warrior. He'd expected to be a God here. Instead, this little female seemed to command him.

His body burned as his dragon fought to come out.

Goddess knows what she saw, but she backed up, nearly tripping, a familiar look in her eyes. Fear. Fear looked the same in any species. Swallowing back his rage and his desire for her, Kal focused on her and only her. Seeing beyond just the curvy exterior of her. There was so much more.

"What are you?" he asked.

He shook off the last lick of fire on his fingertips.

"I could ask you the same thing," she said.

He stepped forward. "I've answered you. A dragon. From another planet far, far away. Now, what are you?"

She swallowed. "Just a-a witch."

Kal breathed in deep, catching the aroma of her body. A mix of fear, anger, nerves, and the sweet scent of arousal.

He flexed his hands, his muscles tensing.

He couldn't look away. Regardless of the irritation of being changed into some helpless bird, he still wanted her. No one could have explained this to him.

"Not just a witch, I can feel your power," he said.

Energy raged through him at the mere sight of her. His dragon burned hotter and he couldn't control the hunger deep in his soul. The warriors had been sent to find their mates. If they didn't, they would burn brighter and hotter, until one day they couldn't control the energy within them.

The thing was, Kal was pretty damn sure he burned hotter in the presence of this creature, something he didn't think was supposed to happen.

"Your eyes," she said, as she took a step towards him.

He blinked. "What about them?"

She stopped and her scent came to him as the flow of air in the room danced around her.

He didn't look away; she was in his sights. Kal's throat burned dry as the need to taste her surfaced.

"They. I've never seen a shifter's eyes like yours. It's almost like you're on fire."

"I'm a dragon. My soul welcomes the fire. I didn't lie about what I am."

He was supposed to keep the space stuff out of the conversation. Then again, he was supposed to be all powerful and not get bested by some female. She wasn't what he'd expected. The last time his people had been here,

16

humans were still building triangle tombs and worshiping his kind.

Confused, and probably not helpless, she stared at him. No, not helpless. He'd best remember that.

Maddie's lips moved without a sound coming out. She crossed and uncrossed her arms. He loved to watch her move. Goddess, she was sexy. How was he supposed to keep his hands off of her? There were rules. What the fuck were the rules again?

He couldn't remember. Kal watched her mouth, but words weren't what he wanted right now. Kal wanted to know if she tasted as sweet as she smelled.

He wanted to know if her breasts filled his hands. He wanted to know what it would feel like to sink his dick deep within her.

Kal adjusted his stance. Goddess, his dick didn't seem to care much for rules.

Fuck them. Fuck the rules. Fuck the whole plan.

He grabbed her wrist, and tugged her toward him.

"Oh," she said. Her eyes wide in surprise, but she didn't resist.

"I have traveled a very, very long way, Maddie, and I'm hungry."

Maddie locked her eyes onto his, her chest rising and falling quicker and quicker.

"I, the bar. They have food," she whispered.

"I don't want food…" he answered.

Her pulse raced under his touch.

"I don't understand - I'm, what's your name?"

He smirked. She wasn't ignoring him now.

"Kal. My name is Kal, Maddie. My little witch."

His thumb started to trace circles on the inside of her

wrist. He could feel the energy with each beat of her heart. Strong little human.

"You're beautiful," Kal said.

She blinked as if coming back from far away. "No. Not me."

His fire burned, the restraint to keep it under control didn't detract from his raging hard-on. "You will never doubt me when I tell you, you are the most beautiful creature I've ever met."

He watched her throat move as she swallowed, the skin on her neck soft, begging to be tasted.

Leaning down, his mouth inches from her ear, he whispered, "tell me, Maddie, do you want me as much as I want you?"

She let out a small gasp.

He licked the ridge of her ear, trailing his tongue down to the lobe.

She shivered.

"I'll warm you, if you let me."

He liked the salty-sweet of her skin as he savored the taste. The energy within her called out to his dragon. Kal watched as veins of golden fire pulsed where his lips left a trace of his own energy. They started to spiral and spread down her.

"I'm not cold," her words came out on a breath.

Kal liked the way she reacted to him, his own body growing more and more desperate. He should stop, but he didn't want to.

Maddie leaned into him, allowing him to hold her tighter.

"No. Not cold," she repeated.

He smirked.

Maddie's breathing grew uneven. Perhaps being changed

into a chicken was all worth it now that his charm was beginning to work on this little human.

His gaze flicked to a glowing string of lines along her neck. Kal stopped. Markings, first faint, and now growing clearer, burned like rivers of fire down the exposed flesh of her chest, disappearing under her shirt, and spreading down her arms.

He moved back as the fire spread over her.

"Shit."

She closed her eyes, moaning. Only this time it wasn't because of his mouth against her.

"What?" she whispered.

He let her go.

"I. Is that normal?"

The markings he'd expected - at some point. He'd been told his mate would share some of his markings, but what the fuck was burning within her? She looked like... well, fuck. She looked like she was burning from the inside out.

He searched his soul. His dragon thrashed within, demanding release.

Not yet.

"Oh," she gasped.

"So, that's not normal?" Kal asked.

She shook her hands and waved her arms.

"God, no. What did you do? I've never seen my magic do this. Crap." Her fingers pulled at the shirt against her, fanning it. "Hot. I'm so hot. Son of a- oh, my God!"

Without another word she tore out the door and down a hall, the scent of char wafting towards him.

Like a damn idiot he stood there, confused as fuck. Did he follow? Where did she go?

Stupidity taking a backseat, he took off down the hall, the scent of her mixed with the scent of smoldering flame.

Kal stopped as he stepped from the hall back to the bar he remembered.

"Maddie?" he said, scanning the space.

The bartender glared at him. "She's here." Rolling her eyes, Ellen pointed down behind the bar.

Taking one more survey of the space, he decided that his brother had deserted him. No other threats appeared. Maddie was all that mattered right now.

He took the floor in six long strides.

"What did you do to her?" asked Ellen.

He braced himself against the bar and leaned over.

He jerked his head back and looked again. "Maddie?"

"Maddie, get your damn head out of my freezer. That's seriously against like every damn health code," said Ellen.

"What have you done to her?" he asked, this time.

"What have I done? I'm not the huge asshole that she just came out of the back room with. I'm guessing you did something," scolded Ellen.

Kal snarled. He didn't like the way this female looked at him.

Ellen laughed. "Is he that hot, Madds?"

She pulled out, steam rising as her skin melted the ice she ran down her skin.

"I'll fix it. Just let me cool down. I'm hot. Is it hot in here?" Maddie rambled.

The bartender grinned at Kal. "I'd be too if I'd just been locked in the office with this one."

He shrunk back as the female licked her lips. Kal would worry about the fact he wanted no other females any longer later, and the fact that Maddie had him worried. He didn't do worry.

"I don't understand, is this normal?" He turned to Ellen.

He needed answers.

Ellen laughed. "What? To burn up like a campfire? No. I mean, we have strange stuff here. But no. Can't say that's normal."

He nodded and started to step away. What the hell should he do?

"Don't you dare leave. Not until you fix me," Maddie said. She dumped a handful of cubes down her shirt.

She closed her eyes. "You have no idea how good that feels."

His dragon began to paw and scratch. His skin rippled. He'd be fucked if she died, but he didn't know what to do.

He listened to his soul; the dragon growling. He would need to pull the fire from her. The fire spoke to him, he could pull it into his soul.

"Maddie, can we please go somewhere more private?"

This wasn't something he understood, but he understood fire. He understood energy. He understood his need to save her. This wasn't part of the mating ritual. It was almost as if she'd absorbed part of him within her and he could only think of one way to get it back.

The warrior within took control as his senses honed in on her heart rate, her breathing, everything faster. Not like before though, not when she had wanted him. This was much too different.

Maddie grabbed a rag and started to toss cubes in it.

"I'll bring this back," she said, placing the bundle against the back of her neck.

Ellen nodded as Maddie took off.

He followed her, she teetered and staggered to a back door. Kal barely caught her as she nearly fell.

"So hot. It's so hot. Help me, Kal."

21

$\mathcal{M}$addie swatted away Kal.

Hot.

She tore at her shirt. Maddie pushed, trying to get away from Kal.

"Maddie. Stop. Please. Let me do as you asked. I can help."

Heck, no. He wasn't coming closer. The heat burned hotter when he touched her.

Holy hell. She backpedaled. Turned around. Reached for the brick wall of the alley. Something, anything. Her magic didn't respond when she called it. Or If it did, she couldn't be sure it knew what she wanted. She didn't know what she wanted. She needed to clear her damn head.

Was this what it felt like to burn at the stake? Thank God, witch trials were long gone. Her body was on fire. Literally. If she started to burn up, it might be a relief. She looked down at her arms spidering with odd markings she'd never seen.

"What did you do, Kal? Is this like an infection? Are you a body snatcher?"

He backed off a bit, but he didn't step away. Probably best in case she fell or fainted.

"What? Body snatcher? That species is extinct if memory serves."

What the hell was wrong with this guy? "No. It's a movie. What the heck are you talking about? Never mind. God, I need a pool. Forget that, I'll take a horse trough. Hell, I'd dunk my own head in a toilet. What is wrong with me?"

She jolted to a stop. Kal stood in front of her.

"Maddie. Stop. You need to let me help."

"Please Kal, get out of my way. I need to cool -"

She gasped as his lips closed on hers and stole the words.

His lips commanded her. The fire burning within her seemed to form a line from her toes to where their bodies touched, ready to take orders.

Sweet relief.

She opened for him as his tongue danced with hers. After a few brief seconds, the pain subsided and the relief he gave her was enough to let her submit to this man. Then, a new heat filled her, this time not painful. Need.

She wound her hands around his neck, pulled him closer, the feel of the leather of his coat annoying to her roaming fingers. Logic burned away as she lost touch with reality and just felt him.

She needed him. She wanted him. A desire so strong, caution blew away on the wind. Was this how it felt to go for it? Take what you wanted? Use the man just as he would use her?

God, please use me.

She trailed her fingers down, running over rock solid abs under a thin tight shirt, brushing over the ridge of his pants, running her index finger along the outline of a massive bulge.

23

Alien, shifter, warlock, who the hell cared if he was a walking gnome right now. She'd let him do whatever the hell he wanted.

His hands reached around and grabbed her ass, lifting her. She obliged and wrapped her legs around his waist, pressing her pelvis against him. Maddie wanted the pressure of him against her core. She needed to feel him.

God, he was hot. Her hands running over the fire seeping out of his clothing, she welcomed the burn. She liked it, and the idea seemed mad.

A groan caught in her throat, her arms encasing his neck as he pushed against her rhythm.

"Wait," he said, pulling away.

She blinked. Twice.

"What? No. You don't say wait. That's not how this works. I'm throwing myself at you. There is no wait."

His lips spread into a grin. "Calm, mate. First, how do you feel?"

"Feel? I feel like I was about to have the best sex of my life and you just cockblocked yourself." Maddie stopped. She was yelling for no good reason other than she was horny. Blowing out a breath, she suddenly realized that she actually did feel better.

A few more deep breaths and Maddie started to regain her senses.

The air around her dry and hot, but not unbearable. It was a desert, but this was the familiar heat she'd expected.

"I'm better -" she said. "Wait, what? Mate? What the what?" Her next breath wouldn't go down past the sandpaper in her throat. No. She heard him wrong. All she'd done is make out with the guy.

"Calm yourself. I'm trying to understand your species."

Her nose crinkled and she could feel the heat rising on her face, this time from anger.

"No. Wait. What did you say before? Go back to the mate thing. You didn't bite me or anything, did you? Goddamn it. You hear about this stuff happening, but no one ever thinks it will be them. Oh, that's it." She squirmed. "Put me down." He held tighter. "Mother? Where the hell are you?"

She stopped as his brow furrowed.

"What, Kal? Don't you look at me like that. Mate. My Ass. "

Kal seemed to be at a loss for words. Good. Serves him right. What a prick. She hadn't even had the opportunity to decide if the sex was good enough to just let him have her as his mate or not. Sure. Just you watch. She'd get the one shifter who sucked in bed or something.

"You are my mate. Are you questioning this? The goddess herself had deemed it so. You see your markings. They match mine."

Maddie narrowed her eyes. "I don't like the sound of this goddess. You think she'd be on the side of all women."

Stretching her arm, she took notice of the tattoos. There were indeed markings. Subtle designs marked her skin where there had been nothing before. Well, hell.

Why did she get the weird stuff? She'd never done anything wrong. She'd always followed the rules, well, except for not marrying her ex. But that hadn't been right. He deserved to be loved. She just didn't, she couldn't. She wouldn't marry him just because it had been expected. She hated predictability. Then again, right now she wasn't sure she enjoyed spontaneity that had fucking tattoos showing up.

Right now, she wasn't a fan. Thirty seconds ago... no. She needed to stay focused.

"I don't understand? Any woman chosen by the goddess is

blessed. She only chooses the strongest, most deserving females to mate a warrior."

"Ha. A warrior? God, you shifters really need to figure out how to live in the twenty-first century. No one has warriors anymore."

Gripping her hands on his shoulders, she tried to release herself from his iron grip.

Something very hard and very notable pressed against her own girly bits and she nearly swallowed her own damn tongue.

"I'm a warrior," his tone stern.

His eyes burned bright, and she swore they changed into something else. A - a dragon? Maybe he wasn't lying.

"You're a shifter, right? You transform into some kind of animal."

He nodded. "By that definition, yes. I am."

Maddie nervously chewed her lower lip. "Okay. We're getting somewhere. So, all right. Honestly now, what are you? Dragon's aren't real."

Maddie swore she could see his chest puff out. Great. Macho ass.

"Never mind. I'll just go home now. Once you put me down."

God, did she really want him to put her down. Maddie shifted and nearly moaned as she rubbed up against him.

Think.

She needed to use her brain. Where the hell was home anyway. She'd come back to Roswell, to this desert town full of weird, strange, and magic because her mom wouldn't stop haunting her damn dreams. She'd only come because, well, losing her show meant she didn't have much to do elsewhere. But, coming here meant that she didn't exactly have a home anymore either. Mom didn't need a house now so where exactly was she going to go?

"Well. This sucks."

Gently he put her down.

As Maddie went to step around him, Kal imprisoned her on either side with his massive arms.

"I think perhaps I have been misled or misinformed on humans. Can we start over?"

Stomping her foot, she shook her head. "Fine. Whatever. I don't have much else going for me right now."

He reached for the now wet rag dripping along the sidewalk.

"I transform into what you would call a dragon. We do exist. We are very, very real." Kal moved in closer. She could smell his natural musk now, something spicy, new, him.

Would it suck to just let him do whatever he wanted? The scent of him seemed like a drug she was already addicted to.

"Just not here on Earth," his words a tickle on her cheek.

Maddie gawked. "You talk as if you are from, well shit. "

He shrugged. "I told you. I am not from around here. I really have a ship and my species is here to find our mates."

He was batshit crazy. Wonderful.

"Okay. Okay. Space. If I believe you. And I am so, not saying I do, why would someone like you have to come here? Are you considered ugly on your planet?"

She paused. Good Lord. If he was the black sheep on his own planet, well hell. Just hell. And he wanted her?

His eyes narrowed. "Mate, you wound me. Do you not find me -" he nuzzled the crook of her neck and the instant pool of need had her crossing her legs. Kal mumbled against her neck, "desirable?"

Her breathing hitched. "Yes. God, yes. But, why me?"

Raising her hands, she ran them through his hair.

"There is no reason. You were simply made for me and I for you. You are my destiny."

She swallowed. "Yes. But why not your own kind?"

A whimpered cry followed his retreat. Why was he going? She liked whatever it was he'd been doing to her neck.

"My kind are rare. We can't find mates on our own planet. This," he paused and kissed her, "is-" another kiss "the only other planet we are compatible with."

Wait, what? Breathing? Check. Words. What had he just said? She wanted him to keep kissing her. No. Answers.

"Stop that."

Another kiss. Her lips tingled.

"Stop what?" he asked.

"That," she said.

Nodding, he started to step away.

Hell no!

Gripping his shirt, she pulled him back.

"No. I mean. Just stop kissing me."

Kal smiled.

"You're telling me you're an alien. A dragon alien? And that somehow I'm it. Like, as in, the it of all its. Like fate just decided that I'm what you have to wake up with every morning for the rest of your life?" She stopped.

"Wait. dragon. Okay - this is Roswell. Let's say I buy the whole alien thing - WTF about the dragon thing. I mean. Seriously."

He held her hand, drawing little patterns against the back of her skin.

"You've heard stories of dragons coming and going throughout history? Where do you think they came from?"

She pressed her lips in a thin line. This was Roswell and

apparently anything was possible, she guessed. Right? She had been chasing ghosts for a living. And her mother wasn't exactly alive.

Okay. She'd bite. "Fine. Prove it."

He reached for his chest and pulled aside the collar of his shirt.

Her mouth went dry. Damn!

Once she regained her senses, her eyes shifted to the tattooed skin on his well-defined pec.

Earth just didn't make men like this.

"This is my dragon," he said, pointing to the tattoo.

"No. That's a picture of a dragon. Okay. So. Yeah. Fine, it's yours."

Maddie stepped outside her anger and frustration. The animal glowed against his skin. Reaching for him, it, whatever, she paused, and then when Kal didn't stop her she traced it with her finger. The creature rippled under her touch. Glancing up at Kal, she saw his eyes were closed.

"Show me," she whispered."Show me who you are."

Kal looked around, and for a moment she doubted that he wasn't crazy and lying to her.

"Not here. Too many chances to be seen. Do you trust me?"

Maddie's first thought was, 'no dumb-shit. I just met you.' Something within her stopped though, and she couldn't say no because, she did trust him. He stopped the burn within her, but replaced it with a new need. Him.

"Yes."

He released the neckline of his shirt and smiled.

Her eyes drifted away from his neck, over his shoulders. He wasn't any less menacing now than he'd been when she'd first seen him, but there was something different that Maddie hadn't noticed. A softness to the hard edges. Maybe she'd been wrong about him. Or maybe his little stint as a chicken had done wonders.

Maddie started to reach for his arm, only to falter. His eyes met hers and she reached for him again. Her hand rested on soft leather, as she just now realized how inappropriately he was dressed for a desert.

"Aren't you hot?" she asked.

He shrugged. "No. I like the heat. Where I come from the planet is much closer to our sun than yours."

Deep breaths.

"Right. I forgot. You're not from around here," she said. "You have a ship." That was more an afterthought than a statement.

Kal nodded. "Yes. I tried to show you the ship earlier."

Rolling her eyes, she snorted. "Right. Okay. Let's just say I buy into this whole alien, not-from-this-planet thing. What are you? Why am I burning up and now have some random ass tattoos?"

"Maddie?"

She started.

Son of a - what now?

A swell of history surfaced at that voice, and her face heated, the voice an unwanted blast from the past.

Slowly, she pivoted. "Hi, Donnie."

Don't make eye contact. Don't do it.

An unwanted emotion, guilt, came right along with that voice as she took him in. He'd meant so much to her past, but he just wasn't her future.

"You're back?"

Maddie bit her lower lip. "Yup."

"I saw your show a while back. Sorry it got cancelled."

The heat of Kal sinking through her clothing reminded her he stood behind her. Like right behind. So close. He could be her future. Unless he was batshit crazy.

Her brain seized for a second. Wait? What? Future? She'd just met him.

But what if her past stood in front of her and her future stood behind?

This was what being stuck in the middle felt like, or maybe a crossroad. She couldn't go back. But what if she couldn't go forward? The flame flickering within her burned brighter at the thoughts of what Kal's lips could be doing right now.

Was it bad, the idea that Kal, her maybe future, could be showing her what the impressive bulge pressing against her back right now felt like buried within her? And all she probably needed to do was say she believed him.

"I see you're not alone," said Donnie.

She shook her head. "What?" Oh right, old boyfriend still talking.

Kal's hand rested against her shoulder.

"No. She is not alone." Kal's words were clipped.

A pain flashed across Donnie's face, one that she swore was familiar, similar to the look when she'd given him back his ring a few years ago.

"I see," said Donnie.

Maddie pushed away from Kal. "This is Kal. We just met in the bar."

Okay. That sounded bad.

"I must have drank something that didn't agree with me. He was just helping."

A deep crimson snaked its way past Donnie's collar, up his neck, to his face. "You don't have to lie to me, Maddie. I deserve better than that."

Her eyes widened. "I'm not lying though. I don't know what's wrong with me. I don't feel right. Kal helped me."

A warmth spiraled over her skin as she remembered just how Kal had helped her.

Maddie couldn't figure out the look that passed over Donnie's face.

"Are you okay?" she asked.

He pointed to her. "What are those? Are those new tattoos? What, you dump me and find some, some moron on steroids and suddenly you're a whole new Maddie?"

She stepped back, stopped by the Kal-wall.

"What? No." Looking down, she saw the tattoos again.

"No. These. I don't know what they are. They just appeared today, in fact."

Kal huffed. God, she hoped he'd just shut up.

"She's mine. Those marks are for me."

Maddie squeezed her eyes closed. So much for him just shutting up.

"You just met him today? Really, Maddie? I thought when Ellen called and told me you were back, it was a sign. She didn't mention that you were here with someone."

Deep breaths.

"I did just meet him. I swear. Kal, tell him."

Kal's grip tightened. "We just met, but her soul knows me. Time is merely a detail humans invented, a revolution around the sun. It means nothing to fate."

Oh, God. That wasn't what Donnie needed to hear.

Opening her eyes, she focused on her ex.

A vein in his forehead was popping out. Donnie wasn't bad looking, but really, compared to Kal he lacked something. Poor guy didn't deserve this.

"That sounds like a load of crap from a man who is relying

on his looks to get someone like Maddie. In time, she'll see the truth and -" he broke off.

This time it was her turn to look at him bug-eyed. Oh, he didn't just go there.

"And what, Donnie? Please, finish that statement."

His mouth opened and closed. "Look, Maddie." He took a step closer and Kal's arm found its way around her chest, hugging her close. Protective, almost.

"Maddie. We're meant to be. I know we are. I've waited this long, I can wait a little longer. You're back here. That's got to be a sign."

Tilting her head, she glared. "Please, Donnie. Stop. I never wrote you. I never called. I told you that you deserve someone better. Someone who would love you as much as you love them. Stop waiting for me. There's no reason to. Even if this Kal thing isn't forever -"

She hiccuped on her last word. The heat within her burned hotter at the mention of his name.

"It is forever, Maddie," Kal whispered into her ear. Those words traveled down through her, straight to her core. Oh, Lord. Forever? Right now she'd settle for a quick minute. Crossing her legs, Maddie tried to control the pulsing need.

Blowing out a breath, she focused on Donnie, the person in front of her that kept her from scratching an itch he'd never inspired.

Nope. She didn't love Donnie, not like a girlfriend should. She didn't love the pain behind his eyes either. Maddie would do what she needed to look out for herself, and Donnie was a casualty. She didn't want to be the reason anyone hurt. She didn't want to be in charge of someone else's well-being, or their happiness.

No one could make you happy except yourself. Wasn't that

what she'd learned about everything in her life? Her mother? And right now her happiness could hinge on the crazy alien guy behind her. Or, at least soul-bending ache to have him sweating on top of her.

There was the heat again.

Breathe.

His grip didn't release, his arm still over her chest, holding her close.

Running a finger over the skin on his hand, the only part of him not covered by his jacket, she sighed at the relief. Why? Maybe fate had it right. The heat seemed to jump between them.

Kal's next words reached through her haze.

"Maddie is no longer available, human."

Kal pulled her back as he stepped around her. "You will wait an eternity for her, and even then her heart will remain mine and I will forever be hers. You can't win this."

"No. No, Kal."

Why was he provoking Donnie?

The air grew heavy as she breathed in. Too much. It was too much. Gasps of air, all she got in as she tried to wrap her head around reality.

It was okay. She was in control. She would remain in control. She'd be fine. But no. No. She couldn't rely on someone else. She broke hearts. She didn't save her mom. She couldn't love Donnie. She couldn't keep her show afloat and ensure all her cast had jobs.

The familiar darkness that followed her everywhere flowed over her, thick and heavy. A blanket of anxiety folded itself around her, choking out rational thought.

Maybe you are in control of your own happiness, but what if others relied on you? No. She couldn't.

Gasping in a breath, Kal's words were deadly serious. But how could he say any of that? What if he was wrong? She wouldn't be his - because, what if she couldn't? What if she wasn't capable of being anyone's?

Anxiety swooped in like a vulture stealing the last of her calm. Pushing off Kal's hand and ignoring the pleas of Donnie, she ran.

$\mathcal{H}$is dragon snarled within him. Kal let out a growl. This human male would pay.

They could still smell her scent in the air, hear her footfalls traveling farther away. His mate was leaving him, and it was all this little pest's fault.

Kal and his dragon turned their attention to Donnie. Kal fought to remain in control for the moment. He rolled his head side to side. The tension of keeping his dragon penned was enough to test even his strength right now.

They would go after Maddie as soon as he fixed the Donnie issue. Neutralize the enemy. The sun was no longer above them; the sky darkening. Good. Fewer people to see when he lost the battle against the shift.

"Donnie. I suggest you run while you still can." His voice grew deeper as the dragon started to push his way out.

The weasel of a man sneered. "No. I'm not losing her again."

Kal threw his head back and laughed. Tinges of red and orange streaked the horizon. It reminded him of home, and home would never be the same if he didn't get her to go with him. This Donnie might be an obstacle, whether he liked it or not. Grinding his teeth together, Kal bit back a roar of anger.

The leather of his jacket stretched at the seams as he strained, his muscles burning in restraint as his dragon fought to come out and play. The beast was done with Kal's patience.

No. Not yet.

Compromise, if one compromised with a dragon.

Kal's attention focused on the enemy.

"Look what you did to her," Donnie yelled. "I don't know what you expect out of Maddie, but she's not as strong as she looks. If you think she'll zap you a million dollars or something, then you've got the wrong witch."

Kal ground his molars as his skin scaled up. "I expect nothing of her. She is mine as I am hers. She owes me nothing. I will live to please her." He smirked. "Far better than a small human like you could do."

Goddess, if she'd only let him.

Kal squared his shoulders as his dragon began to beat his wings within their soul. They hadn't found a worthy opponent on this planet, not yet anyhow. Would this Donnie be worthy? Kal chuckled, no, it was doubtful. Donnie was nearly a mouse.

"Don't you laugh at me. You have no idea what you're dealing with. Besides, everyone's a little human here. What makes you think you're better? Get over yourself. You know drugs aren't the answer. Women aren't stupid. Maddie isn't stupid. Maybe you look like, well, what you look like now. Everyone knows that most guys like you can't think your way out of a paper bag," Donnie spouted.

Kal ignored Donnie as he listened, trying to pinpoint

Maddie and realizing he couldn't hear her footfalls anymore. This was taking too long.

"I don't have time for a small human right now. Go do what you will. I need to track down Maddie, and you will go away. You will not be following my mate any further from here on out."

Kal summoned the dragon, letting their senses reach for her. He hadn't officially mated her, but they knew her. He could smell her, feel her. Her magic called to him and his to her.

"What the hell gives you the right to claim her? That's not how marriage works around here."

Kal whipped his head back to the annoying gnat of a human. The stupid male was still here.

Kal rolled his eyes as he looked down at Donnie. The little man had actually come closer. "You play a dangerous game, human," Kal said.

"Listen here. No matter what you are, don't you dare think you're better than me. You fucking shifters. Thinking all women are yours for the taking. Someone needs to teach you assholes a lesson."

Kal took another step forward and the muscles of his arms corded as he let talons rip from his hands.

Control yourself, dragon.

Kal was forbidden to reveal his true form. Shifter it was, for now. He would go with shifter.

"And, I suppose you're the mundane human to teach me?"

Kal enjoyed watching the man's skin burn red in anger. He could smell the spicy scents of rage.

"I'm half Fae, you asshole. My father was a guard in the Fae courts."

Kal shrugged. He knew of stories of the Fae, another creature that frequented humans throughout history. Fascinating to see they too needed this species.

"Should that make me afraid?"

Donnie didn't back away.

Interesting.

Perhaps this would be more entertaining than expected. Kal stepped forward, stopping a foot away from him, the darkness of dusk taking over.

Time to play, little mouse.

Kal knew Donnie would see him shift. Perhaps he'd see enough to frighten the halfling.

He flexed his shoulders, letting the ripple of the magic control him, his dragon clamoring to come out.

"What the hell are you?" Donnie asked.

"Perhaps you'd like to find out? Show me what being part Fae really means? If you think you are worthy."

Kal advanced on him as his teeth began to morph into those of his dragon.

Donnie scowled. "Maybe I don't glow like you or have some freaky-ass eyes, but I don't need to prove myself to you. She will come back to me."

Kal grew hot as his anger boiled within. No one would touch his mate.

Leaning in, he whispered his next words while he still could, before the dragon fully emerged. "You touch her and you will die." Standing to his full height, he glared down at Donnie.

"You kill me and she will never forgive you, shifter. It doesn't matter what you are. She loves me."

Kal reached out to grab Donnie and scowled as his grip came up with air.

"I told you I'm not just human. I'm very fast. Perhaps you should take those fucking gym muscles and leave town."

A game. They liked games.

"She may love you. Most humans love pets."

Kal grinned as he let his dragon take hold. His jaw began to protrude, making room for his razor-sharp teeth. His voice grew deeper, his skin fully morphed and fell away into scales as they grew in size.

"What the fuck?" Donnie stuttered. He retreated until his back hit the door to the bar with a metallic thud. Reaching for the doorknob, his hand fumbled. Kal folded forward onto all fours.

Fear was something Kal could work with.

Drool dripped from their dragon mouth, and just as they approached, Donnie ripped open the door. His last words were muffled as the door began to close, "you're not winning this one. I'll be back."

The deep rumble of the dragon's voice vibrated as they laughed. Right. He'd be back, and Kal would be ready all the same.

The dark of night fell, his dragon shaking off the long trip cooped up within Kal's soul. Their tail whipped back and forth. Did they wait for the little man to come back? Choices, choices.

Shitty human. Thinking he could beat us. Now for the hunt.

The dragon laughed and then pulled their large body around to face the direction of Maddie's scent.

Yes. Let's go find her.

Using the power of their rear legs, they shot up into the darkening sky. Kal allowed the dragon to take over as they searched the darkening streets. He needed to find her. How many hours before he had to report back? Not like he would report back without her. No. Kal refused to step back on that damn ship without her.

Kal could sense his brothers, all different directions. They needed to focus on the mission.

He wondered how the rest were faring, although right now he couldn't deal with that. Not until he found her. This was more than saving his own soul.

The dragon soared through the air. Not even the freedom of the skies could distract from the gnawing ache he'd never felt. Not until Maddie.

His dragon kept their senses open. She wasn't far.

Soaring above the humans, they tried to remain far enough as to not attract attention. Streets emptied as the darkness grew. If they didn't need to worry about the IGF, Intergalactic Force, finding them on an unsanctioned mission, they had to worry about mass hysteria breaking out on the planet. Shitty choices. Kal had to worry about space police that thought a lot about themselves or his soul bursting into flames. Just another fun week.

The wind parted around him as he searched for her. His dragon sniffed the air, and snorted out. Not the same as home, so many new scents and not all good. A faint trail caught their attention closer to the ground. They could feel her, but now they could see a trail of her own magic. So many threads here. But this was Maddie.

A pulse within his head had his dragon squeezing their eyes shut. His powers grew every day, as they should. The problem was, if he had no balance to his fire, someday he'd burn too bright to exist outside his dragon's form.

Yes, time was running out for them all.

Time was the enemy.

She was close, her presence the only thing breaking past

this new pain. He glanced down, trying to make out her figure, the tattoos visible from his vantage point.

He wouldn't worry about anything but her right now. The Amit goddess's gifts were both a curse and a blessing. If they found their mates, the curse wouldn't matter anymore. Maddie would balance out power, help him control his curse.

Swooping down as he spotted the invisible trail, she was so close he could practically feel her in his arms again. What should he do though?

Kal was supposed to get what he wanted. Earth woman should have worshiped him, and instead, Maddie seemed immune to his charms. He thought back to his own mother and tried to envision how his father had acted around her. It had been a few too many years. His father, killed in one of the many battles that raged through the solar system. A great reminder they weren't gods. Right. Way to see the world as a half-full glass.

Kal turned towards the ground. She sat in a small park. He wouldn't blend in here, not well, hopefully he could reach the ground before anyone noticed. Thankfully, there were no lights. Maddie was the only beacon he'd need.

Straining his hearing as his massive paws hit the ground, Kal could make out her voice.

Kal crouched forward, not willing to shift yet. Not until he knew there were no new threats.

The air smelled of wood. He slid a paw through the loose chips at his feet and sniffed the ground. Odd that they put wood on the ground. He took a step closer. A small bug flitted around his head. He snorted at it and paused as he heard her speak.

"Mother, where are you?"

Watching, he stood still. She twirled around in a circle and yelled to the air.

There was no one. Who was she talking to?

The dragon's eyes looked for heat signatures. Nothing. Narrowing his eyes at a sparkle of magic within the air, they stepped back again. Odd planet indeed.

He wanted to shift back, but this place confused him, and Kal would be damned if he let something unseen get the best of them.

Maybe though, staying in this form would have him screwing things up less too. The dragon chuckled. Remaining in this form, he couldn't say anything to piss off Maddie.

They lowered themselves down, crouched on their front paws and waited. The dragon strained his neck further, curious at the sparkling in the air. What was it?

Maddie turned around again. She wiped at her face and finally stopped talking, her focus on the same spot he studied. This magic was different from Maddie's.

They waited

The dragon enjoyed this game. He enjoyed being out and free. Kal didn't like it though. The only thing this dumbass dragon did was act on instinct and right now, instinct had done nothing but screw up something with their future mate.

Shit.

5

"Mother? Where the hell are you?"

The pain in her chest twisted like a rubber band around her rib cage. Too tight.

The emptiness. God, the emptiness. She'd run far away, or as far as she could before her body protested. The emptiness had dulled, or maybe the pain from her body and the unexpected exercise overpowered it.

Maddie gulped at air like a fish. She couldn't get it in. "Mom?" She screamed. Nothing. So much nothing. Who knew silence could be so deafening? Her mom was here somewhere. She'd called her here.

Just like her, make her daughter come, and then be cryptic.

Her mom would come though. Any minute now. Because she always came. Why wouldn't she? The hope that, at some point, Maddie wouldn't feel this stab of pain and sadness died as she stood here realizing she'd never lose the hope to see her mom. The pain of losing her mother filtered back in. It had never really left, but the stabbing ache had been so much easier to ignore when she wasn't here.

Maddie was used to being alone, but when she was here, home, she had to face her reality. Alone. God, maybe that had been one more reason she'd left Donnie. He hadn't filled the void, but it had never felt like this before.

Maddie couldn't breathe. Couldn't get the air in past the tightness, the burning of her lungs, the pain in her chest that had nothing to do with running away. Donnie's face still looked betrayed. Time apparently didn't heal all wounds, not his. Not hers. Too bad they were both very different wounds.

She pressed her palm to her chest trying to force the panic down, or maybe the air in. She didn't know.

How could Donnie not have moved on yet? How had she been able to ruin his life simply by following her own destiny? Her mother had said that Donnie wasn't right. Her mom had sworn she'd tell Donnie the same once Maddie had gone.

"Mother? Show yourself. Fix this. Fix something."

Honestly? Right now, Donnie wasn't really why she was upset. Was it? No.

Wind blew by, tickling the hairs on her arms, but nothing told her mother was showing.

Maddie backpedaled, wandering without a purpose until she backed into a swing. Mindlessly she sat, pushing her tiptoes against the wood chips, rocking herself. A playground. A place to be happy. Fitting she stopped here, she supposed.

Alone. Always alone.

She sat swinging back and forth, back and forth. When was the last time she'd gone to a park? Years.

The wind blowing through her hair, the cool night air, her legs pumping in and out making her go higher and higher. There was nothing.

There was no grasping her past, not that she wanted to go back.

Closing her eyes, she felt nothing. Numb, finally.

Her skin began to itch again as her magic started to jump. So much for that.

As she came back down, the swing moving back up, she ignored the needy magic. Maybe she could figure out where she'd been and where she needed to go.

Of course she ran into her ex. Like the guilt of dumping him a few months from their wedding would have gone away. She didn't miss him, but she didn't like that she'd hurt him.

The world flew by as the swing came back down and swung back up. Her ex had been one of her first attempts as an adult to defy her mother's know-it-all attitude. She'd been so sick of her mom spoiling everything, all the time.

That date won't work or, he's not right for you.

Of course, she was always right, Maddie had just wanted to live her own life. Just once in her life Maddie had wanted to date blindly and think just maybe he could be the right one. Donnie had been sweet and kind. He'd been a great guy and there had been no reason for her to say no.

Then her mother died, and the emptiness set in. The anger.

Maddie let her hair fly forward and fly behind her with each tilt of the swing. The wind cooled the heat starting to burn against her skin again. No, no. She didn't need that again. Breathing around it, she conjured up a colder wind and let it blow over her. Better. For now.

Her lips tingled with memories of Kal. She wanted him, but no one fell in love in minutes. He had been real though, hadn't he? Where was her mom now to tell her it wouldn't work? Only deep down Maddie knew that her mother wouldn't say that. Not this time. Or maybe she would and that scared Maddie more. What if this, this hunger for Kal wasn't the real thing?

She needed to push it all away, only she couldn't. This town brought all the memories of her mother's funeral back, flooding her. The memories of what her mother hadn't done. She'd refused to do anything to stop her death. God, that was her mother in a nutshell. She believed everything she saw and decided long ago that there was little reason to fight the visions. Maddie wondered if her mother had gone off the deep end right around when her father had returned to hell. Her mother had seen him leaving and couldn't find any way to stop it. Demons, unpredictable shits.

Dust picked up in the surrounding air, the light breeze disrupting, and then blowing more fiercely as she closed her eyes against the churning sand.

Unfamiliar sounds filled the park, and she dragged her feet against the wood chips on the ground to slow the swing. Maddie peeked out of one eye. She opened both eyes when nothing flew at her and looked into the dark.

The glow of her skin broke the pitch of the night, the tattoos filling in like rivers of fire. As she looked away from her own skin, she caught the glimpse of a large animal. An animal that glowed in markings. A beast that strangely resembled something that didn't exist. Her eyes grew wider, taking him in. Or did they? Because he was a massive dragon.

What the hell. Dragons. They were real.

She blinked. Dragons weren't real. Maddie stood, her hands still on the chains. Slowly she took a step, mesmerized by the beast. Releasing the cold metal of the chain, Maddie started walking, tripping over uneven ground.

Amazing.

The dragon started to approach her, and she tried to scurry back. What the hell?

Her body started to burn hot again, but her fear kept the focus on surviving. How in the hell was a dragon... she stopped, the panic slipping away as he came closer.

Those eyes.

Maddie sucked in air, quieting her panic.

"Kal?"

The dragon snuffed, yes or no, she wasn't sure. When he didn't attack, she figured it was a yes.

"Okay. So, is that a yes?"

A nervous laugh escaped. "A dragon. How many dragons could there be? Of course it's you." Recalling the morning, she tried to remember another guy with Kal. Okay, so maybe there were two. But still, those eyes.

"I know it's you."

Standing and dusting her butt off, Maddie took a deep breath. Sliding one foot forward, she reached out her hand, hesitation pulling her back. Glancing around, she questioned her sanity. What if she'd just made Kal up and now this, a dragon? Was her mind so desperate to feel something, it could make any of this up?

Heat swirled around her, a trickle of sweat tickling her temple.

Not now.

Maddie could live her entire life without any more damn hot flashes. This needed to wait until she could understand him, Kal. The dragon shifted and made an impatient huff.

"Oh, just shut it. Excuse me for being a little skeptical. Have you seen your teeth?"

The stupid shit spread his lips and gave her a better view.

"I'm not a dentist. I don't need to see them." Rolling her

eyes, she walked up to him. At least Maddie was sure it was Kal now.

Breathing past the burning starting behind her eyes, she pushed forward. What would he feel like?

This was real.

This was all insane. Then again, was it? Witches, vampires, shifters, ghosts, Fae, shit she hadn't ever heard of, all existed. Why was a dragon so hard to wrap her head around?

"Maddie sweetheart, just pet the man."

She jumped and looked up. "Great timing, Mom."

Even Kal's dragon stretched his neck and shrunk back in confusion.

"This is my mother, Kal. Mom, this is uh, Kal."

Her mother floated closer, inspecting the dragon. "I see. Interesting. I mean, I saw him. But, this. Well, he's just wonderful, isn't he? Sort of like an extra large scaly dog."

The dragon growled.

"I don't think Kal appreciates that." Maddie stepped closer, and the burning increased. She shook her hands, praying the fire raging through her veins would stop. It needed to stop long enough for her to talk to her mother. Maddie tried to magic up some ice. Holy hell. This fire thing needed to stop.

"Oh, hush sweet-pea. Kal here knows as well as I do that he's as harmless as a house pet around you."

Maddie reached her hand out instinctually, laying it against him, her mother's words stopping her train of thought.

"I think that's rude to a shifter. Whatever. You weren't normal when you were alive, like you're going to change now that you're a ghost."

Her mother laughed, the sound pulling at old memories,

the memories where she realized just how much she missed her mom, and how running wouldn't have changed that.

"All right, Mom. Why did you call me back here?"

Maddie wanted the answer - but as she said it, her vision blurred. Fanning herself, she licked her lips, and fought the need to lie down.

Breathing in cool air did nothing to cool her. The world seemed to shift for a moment. Her legs grew weak with each passing second. Swallowing against the exhaustion washing over her, she blinked and leaned on Kal for support.

"Isn't it obvious? They finally arrived, my dear. Maddie, all this time I wanted you to realize your fate simply wasn't here, yet."

Maddie blinked away the blurriness in her eyes.

"You're kidding me. You called me back here because of him?"

Her mother floated closer and made a half-hearted attempt at brushing Maddie's hair back.

"I called you back because I'm worried about you. You don't come to visit much. You're unhappy."

Screaming sounded good right now. Maddie wanted to shake her mother, if you could shake something without a body.

"Mother! I'm unhappy because you died, and you didn't even try to stop it. I'm unhappy because all my life you've told me what my destiny wasn't and then you didn't even try to save yourself."

Maddie leaned into Kal, instinct driving her to find him, a solid force, a force that wouldn't leave her.

She glanced back. Was that the truth? Was that how she actually felt? Or was she just trying to find a reason for her need?

Maddie focused on standing as a wave of heat raged through her.

"I understand, sweetheart. I do. But something you've never understood is that you can't always change the future. You always thought I hadn't tried to see all options, and in the end, this was the easiest for you. My soul survived, I'm still here for you."

Maddie fought the pressure behind her eyes. Son of a bitch, she would not cry. It had been two years. She wouldn't cry.

"I don't need a ghost. I need you. A ghost can leave me again. I can't lose you again, and again. The one thing I know is ghosts."

Kal circled his head around, encasing Maddie in the crook. Strength. A flash of heat had her head swimming again.

No. Not now.

"Love, he's the reason I've hung around. He's my unfinished business. I couldn't leave until my baby had finally found the right one. But, you're right. Someday I'd like to rest. But not until you're safe."

Resting her free hand on her chest, Maddie focused on the beating of her heart and not the heat coursing through her like a wildfire at the height of a drought. She focused on the rock of a- well hell, the dragon holding her safely near him.

"Kal, dear. Please shift back. You found her, now put the dragon away for a while. You can't get through this town looking like that, anyway."

Maddie stepped away as his body shifted and moved away. The surrounding air boiled. Even in his absence, she couldn't cool. Maddie pulled at the neck of her shirt. She had the thought that his retreat left her a few degrees hotter.

Her powers were useless against this magic. Focusing on

Kal, the dragon, she could feel them, they were there. Close. Focus on that.

No. Too hot. Maddie called the cool breezes again, praying that this time the spell would be enough.

Just as quickly as the dragon had moved away, a strong body pressed against her.

Slowly she turned, battling the pain spiking within her body.

If moving had been a mistake, seeing Kal in all his glory had been the best decision she'd ever make for the rest of her life. Maddie's eyes widened. Yeah, okay. He had muscles in places she didn't know had muscles.

Oh God.

Was it possible for it to be hotter? Quickly she cast her eyes to the sky. But, then she peeked again. Damn it.

Her eyes followed down his body, one inch at a time. Hot. So hot. Her, him. Who the hell knew at that exact moment.

There was one muscle that Maddie couldn't unsee. She didn't want to unsee it.

Shit. Wait.

Oh God. Nope. Burned into her brain forever.

Maddie looked again.

"Don't worry, dear. I don't think he has any scruples over you looking." Her mother floated around Maddie and Kal. "My, my, my. Fate really likes you, my dear. He was worth waiting for, don't you agree?"

"Mother!" Maddie squeaked.

The ghost sauntered a few feet away. "Good Lord, Maddie. I'm dead, not nonexistent. Even I can enjoy a good male specimen. Tell him to stay clear of cemeteries though. Good Lord, he could bring new life to some of those corpses."

Her face heated, or maybe it was the stupid fire raging in

her body rather than her mother's embarrassing words. This was one of those high school moments where you just wanted the floor to suck you up.

"Mother. Stop."

Maybe her demon father could swallow her up right now.

"Think of it as research, sweetheart. I can't leave my daughter with someone, well, someone like your ex. He would not please you, ever."

Yup. Swallow her right now. "Mother. Please stop. I can't. No mother should see their future son-in-law's junk."

Kal stopped in front of her. Maddie tried to look away. She tried to look over his shoulder. She tried not to stare at him, but for crap's sake. She wanted to jump him.

"I understand the word future. Son-in-law though?" Kal asked.

Her eyes met his. "I uh. No. It was just a figure of speech. You don't worry about it."

Shit. Shit. Shit. She'd really just implied that maybe he had a future with her. And, maybe he did. Maybe she should listen to her damn mom this time. Then again.

A wave of dizziness hit her. The fire growing.

So hot. Boiling.

Kal's arms jetted out towards her, catching Maddie before she fell.

Her arms had started to shake as she reached out to him. Kal's form came in and out of focus. The only comfort was the strong grip he placed around her. At least she wouldn't fall if her legs gave out.

"You're all right, mate?"

"I. Maybe? Just give me a second."

Kal placed a hand over her head and closed his eyes. She

took a deep breath for the first time in forever. The searing pain behind her eyes subsided to a dull roar.

"Better?" Kal asked.

She blinked. "Yes. A little. I can stand now."

"Maddie dear, accept your fate so I can rest. Accept him, because seriously, if you don't someone else will. I mean… I think I can feel my heart beating."

"Mother."

Her mom's ghost chuckled.

"You don't have to sell me on him. If he wants me, then he will figure out how to win me."

His arm slipped around her, pulling her tight. Her body relaxed, and tingles of something she couldn't identify followed. Hell, he didn't have to work that hard.

"Well love, sometimes I feel like you failed to see that I knew best. I want you to make the right choice, just for once."

Maddie went to put her mother in her place, but all that came out was a puff of air as her body cranked up the heat and took her back a step. Head to toe the fire burned. Maybe she looked cool, glowing, but right now all she could think of was the pain.

"Mom?" She tried to call out. The blaze burning a destructive trail through her veins intensified. Everything faded around them.

A reprieve from the pain came along her arm where Kal touched her.

"Maddie?"

Kal's voice broke through her agony. He kissed her earlier and made it all better, or well, slightly better.

Blindly she reached for his face.

"Kiss me."

6

*H*esitation wasn't something he knew, and now was not the time to feel a new and human emotion. Doubt. What if he couldn't save her? No, there was no room for this.

Kal pressed his lips to hers, wrapping his arms around her soft curves. The dragon quieted for a moment as they dragged in the heat, a high from magic coursing through his veins. He didn't have to look to know that his tattoos were burning brighter like a fire being stoked. His dragon grew within him, stretching with energy.

Through the haze of the power, he realized something was still wrong. He breathed her in. Her scent changed. Singed. It was then that Kal felt the blaze of Maddie's skin. This wasn't right. His soul pulled in the power burning within her, stronger, faster.

In one motion he tightened his grip around her as she went limp. Pulling his lips from hers, he called out. "Maddie?" Her body was near lifeless.

The heat singed even through her clothes as he lifted her.

What the hell was going on? No one had warned them, him, that humans could be affected by their power. None of the humans in all the years of warriors finding mates had ever done this. They were supposed to find their mate, and their mate was supposed to be able to handle the power once the ritual had been completed.

Words. All just words. His dragon would know her the second he saw her. She would be able to survive his fire. She would wear his markings. All the rules and yet she followed almost none of them. The markings dancing over her skin would have blinded him had he not been what he was. This wasn't right. It was as if she were the sun, and that wasn't possible. No one could survive that.

"Shit."

He kissed her again, but this time Maddie didn't respond. He breathed in, pulling the magic from her again and again, trying to rid her of his cursed power.

"Kal, although I appreciate your concern for my daughter, this isn't working. Come with me, dear boy."

He looked over his shoulder and saw the ghost.

His heart beat faster than the flapping of his wings against a hurricane solar storm.

"Maddie? Answer me." He couldn't lose her. Not now, not ever. He'd just found her. His nightmares crashed in around him, his greatest fears manifesting. Failure to save his mate. He wasn't dreaming though, this was real.

Kal moved quickly , careful to keep Maddie supported.

This ghost thing made no sense, but Maddie loved her. He would trust her too.

"Help me save her. I will do anything. I'm meant to protect her, my mate. I can't lose her. Please."

Kal stood there, waiting for instructions. Helpless. He had

no idea where to go. The ship was too far and his brothers wouldn't have known what to do, anyway.

"She'll be fine. Don't take too long though. My daughter, she's special. Far different from anything you were expecting, I would think."

Maddie started to sweat in his arms, the glowing of the tattoos too bright.

"Maddie's Mom, take me wherever I need to go. I will do anything."

The ghost floated a few feet in front of him. "Follow me. Quickly. "

He did as told, his bare feet pulling in the cold of the ground as they ran. Kal hated the cold, but he needed to cool her down. He needed to cool his Maddie, even if the cold caused him to ache.

"Please. Can we go faster?"

Without looking up, Kal followed the shift in magic in the air as the ghost moved.

"Only another block."

Kal, a god-like creature, and yet right now he felt helpless as Maddie burned up in his arms.

"Here. This is the house. I've kept it knowing she'd return soon enough."

Kal took the steps two by two before he hit the porch.

"Stop, young man," the ghost yelled.

He paused. "What?"

She floated to the right, to a small swing.

"The key is under here, please do not break down that door."

He glanced over, confused. What key? Didn't they have some kind of recognition software? God, what kind of planet was this? He couldn't wait to go home to technology.

"How does one use this key?"

She rolled her eyes at him. No one was afraid of him either. He hated this planet right now. "Kal, I can see the future. Now, stop wasting time and get the key."

He supported Maddie the best he could as he bent to grab the key. She mumbled something as her feet touched the porch, her weight almost completely on him.

"Kal, before you take my daughter in, know something. You will need to take her away from here. And soon. Our planet has its own problems. Its own villains and unfortunately I can see them coming. Please protect her. She doesn't have any real reason to stay here, anyway. Make that clear to her. She has nothing to stay for."

Kal nodded as he scooped her up once again. Holding up the key, he took the porch in two long strides only to end up glaring at the door.

"You put it in that hole right there. I hope you are better at this mating thing than you are at locks."

Kal growled.

"Calm down. It was a joke. Put the key there and turn."

He fumbled with the tiny key as he tried to get it into the keyhole.

Finally, the knob turned, and he burst through the entrance.

"This is my cue. I'll come back to say goodbye later. Protect her."

"With my life," he responded and kicked at the primitive piece of wood.

The door slammed shut, leaving them in a deafening silence. Alone. Now what?

The house smelled clean, old, and empty. No threats, just his Maddie. What did he do? Where was he supposed to take her? The darkness didn't hurt his sight. He could make out shadows, doorways.

The words from Maddie's mom haunted him as he looked down the hall. The thought that perhaps she wouldn't want to leave had never entered his mind. He hadn't been prepared for that response.

Maddie moaned, pulling him to the present.

His dragon paced, his soul suddenly felt cramped and this body no longer big enough for either.

Kal pulled her in tighter and tried to call the heat from her. The lick of fire flowed through his bloodstream, a welcome and familiar searing running its natural course. It wasn't enough though.

Maddie opened her eyes as he glanced down at her.

"Where are you taking me?" her voice weak.

"A bed."

He shivered as her fingers ran over the skin of his chest. He could feel her heartbeat as the heat thrummed from her fingers to him. This wasn't fast enough. He wasn't helping enough. Something had to give. She'd be dead if he didn't figure out this dark magic.

"Do you understand why you are so hot?" He met her weak gaze. "Do you know why your magic has you damn near incinerating?"

"I'm a witch and my powers draw from the surrounding elements. I, I think I'm absorbing your power."

She'd closed her eyes again. He didn't understand her magic, but she needed him.

A hall. It had to go somewhere. The couch to the right caught his attention, but there was no way he could do what he needed to, there.

Kal knew what he needed to do. His dragon knew what

they needed to do. Get as much skin contact as possible. Draw the magic from her quickly, and that meant touching as much of her as possible. He would save her. He would do what he needed to, no matter what, to save her.

Kal took off down the hall, Maddie secure in his hold.

The thud and crack of each door he kicked broke the quiet. Bathroom, closet, and finally, pushing open the last door on the left, he'd found something he could use.

A squeak and slow drag of doors settling the aftermath of storm Kal. He'd finally found what he wanted. Maddie's eyes opened.

"Where are we? It looks like…" she trailed off.

"I don't know. But your mother brought me here."

"I'm going to lay you down now."

A weak grip tried to wrap its way around his arm.

"No. Don't leave me," she said.

Gently placing her on the bed, Kal's dragon paced.

"I'm not leaving you."

His skin prickled as he allowed the dragon some freedom. Maybe he knew more than Kal's human form did right now. She blinked at him several times.

"What is the strange light?" she asked.

The orange glow bounced off walls.

"It's you. Your skin is glowing."

He strained to hear her. "My tattoos?"

Kal shook his head. "No. Your entire body."

"Where are we again? Is this your ship? I thought that was a cheesy line."

Kal hated that she was so out of it. That made this even more complicated.

"No. This is not my ship and no, it was not a line. This is your house."

He watched her try to sit up. The sweat dotting her forehead said it all.

"Don't move. I have to cool you down."

He could hear the beat of her heart change. Was this good or bad?

"Like you did earlier?" Maddie asked.

He sat slowly next to her. "Perhaps. Is that okay?"

She started tugging at her shirt.

"I had a smart-ass comment, but right now I don't care what you do to me. I feel like I'm cooking. Just take this fire. Please."

He gripped her hands softly, and leaned in. Her scent stood out to him in a swirling of desert blossoms. He licked his lips, hunger rolling over him. Yes, he would do what he could to cool her down as quickly as possible. Would she allow him to do exactly what he'd wanted to do from the moment he met her?

Her lips parted as Kal leaned in.

"I'm going to kiss you now."

She hiccuped.

Bringing his face closer to hers, he claimed her mouth. His dragon began calling the energy from her. Maybe she commanded a magic he didn't know, but he commanded fire, the sun, the energy of the stars.

Deepening the kiss, her mouth answered the dance and welcomed his tongue as it tasted her.

Kal released her hands and allowed his own to glide down her body, pushing aside her t-shirt. The scent of the air changed as his fingers grazed the skin of her stomach. Kal's magic drew more of the fiery energy and he felt her temperature lowering.

The air, infused with magic and fire, a high, clouding his

head, a euphoric drug. There was only Maddie.

Rivers of fire pulsed through him as he ran his hand down her hip. Pushing closer, he hungered for more. For her.

Maddie wrapped a hand around his neck to pull him to her. Without losing her lips, he adjusted, placing one knee on the bed, the other settling between her legs. Kal's free hand braced himself on the bed.

Desire burned its way through him. His lack of clothing and the excess of her clothing became very unfortunate.

Fuck. He needed her. His hand slid down her hip to her thigh.

She pushed her pelvis up, rubbing against his leg. A moan caught in his throat.

Fuck.

Sweat slicked his skin from restraint.

"Maddie." His breathing heavy, his brain fogged over in desire, he didn't know what the fuck he was trying to ask.

Gripping his face between her palms, she held his attention. "Kal. I need more."

Damn.

His dick jumped for joy.

"More?"

Goddess, let this not be a language barrier. His dick started throbbing.

"Yes. More. I need you to do whatever it is you're doing, but faster."

Treading new territory with Maddie, he paused. Risk. What he believed needed to be done, versus what if it didn't work?

"I need direct contact with your skin." No. He needed all of her. He needed her to submit to him. "I need contact with all of your body."

"Yes," was all she responded.

His eyes scanned her face before he spoke once more. Goddess. He needed to just shut up and take her. That's what his damn dragon thought, anyway.

"You understand what I am asking?"

"Yes."

Maddie pushed her pelvis up against him, her hips wiggling against the bulge in his pants.

He closed his eyes trying to keep himself from coming. Suddenly Maddie growled and pushed him away.

"What?"

"Get off of me and strip, dragon boy."

This was an interesting turn of events indeed, and he sure as fuck didn't need to be told twice.

Gripping the COM on his wrist, he tossed it aside as well as the roll of emergency clothing tied to his ankle.

He pushed up on his knees. "Done"

She paused and damn, didn't he wish she finished undressing.

"Oh. You're quick."

He couldn't help but smile as her eyes roamed over him.

"Dragon, remember? He has no need for clothing."

A hunger sparkled in her eyes, something he'd never seen before. Kal paused and did an inventory. Prey, he felt like prey.

Kal sucked in the air as Maddie shifted. The muscles of his stomach tensed as her wet tongue moistened her beautiful plump lips. She came forward, lowered on all fours. Fuck, he wasn't going to last long at this rate.

"Let me help," he breathed out.

Her face peered up at him, and shit if she wasn't the most beautiful woman he'd ever seen.

Kneeling before him, Maddie took his dick between both hands and started to stroke him. Her tongue darted out, hungry, she licked the tip.

Peering up at him, she smiled. "You are. Don't you feel it?"

Kal didn't have time to blink before her soft lips kissed his belly. Not what he'd expected, but damn if he didn't like the anticipation of where this was going.

His dick twitched, begging for attention as she licked a trail down. His skin grew tight as her touch chased tingles of pleasure replacing the high of magic. He forgot every fucking thing he'd been taught since he was a babe.

Winding his hands through her hair, Kal damn near begged for more as she licked her way down his shaft, back up, circling the head. Maddie's lips soft, warm, and pleading for his cock.

Fuck, me, he thought.

The heat of her breath as she stretched her mouth around him made the world disappear.

Kal was lost to his Maddie.

7

*H*er body tingled and a heat independent of the fire burning through her was new and different. This was her magic, her need.

He tasted of salt and sweat and Kal. She didn't know where the confidence came from, but she liked it. Embraced it as she licked Kal like a dessert.

Swirling her tongue around the tip, licking it, playing with him, teasing him. His breath hitched. This new power was all hers and she would command him any way she wanted.

God knows she wasn't sure how she was going to fit him in her mouth, but she'd try her best. Kal had to be the biggest man she'd ever seen, not that she'd seen that many dicks in her life. If he was her mate, at least fate liked her a lot - maybe. Would she be able to handle him?

Placing her hand over his shaft, she started to stroke - up and down, up and down, licking the sides until he was slick.

Peeking up at his face from where she crouched in front, Maddie liked the way he watched her. Liked the way his eyes rolled in the back of his head as she started to pull him inch by inch.

He was so big and tasted so good. Maddie moaned.

Oh, good God. She needed him. She wanted him.

Her body still burned, and she couldn't separate if it was need, magic, or the flames of his touch. She didn't care.

The muscles between her legs tightened as he ran his hand down her back.

The searing pain dissipated where he touched, or where she touched him.

The muscles between her legs throbbed as one feeling replaced another.

A moan of need found its way out of her throat and his hands tangled in her hair as she moved back and forth along his shaft.

Pulling away, Maddie needed to catch her own breath. As she knelt back, Maddie danced on the edge of need and awe. Kal wasn't just amazing, he wasn't human. No one was this perfect. Her eyes widened as she realized just how large he was fully erect and ready.

He growled as she trailed her finger over the head, and next running down the length.

"Maddie. This." He was breathless. She liked the control she felt over this giant, tough man.

A sense of power flowed through her as his muscles flinched.

"Maddie," he moaned.

She leaned in, kissing the tip.

"Yes?" she answered.

Kal closed his eyes. "Good goddess. Where the hell did you learn to do that?" His breathing came out rough and rapid.

Confidence to continue overrode everything else within

her. This man, a wet dream, even if she wouldn't admit it, and somehow he made her feel like she might be a supermodel. The woman he dreamed about.

Without warning, his eyes flew open, burning orange, pupils elongated. Kal pushed forward, forcing her to move back, forcing her to lie down.

"You are mine, Maddie." He breathed out on a long hard breath.

Crawling up her body, pushing her legs open, spreading her wider and wider, she shivered in anticipation.

"You have one chance to say no, Maddie. One chance before you are mine for eternity."

Her chest fluttered. Eternity sounded like a lot.

Within those eyes though, she saw eternity and liked it. Liked it a lot. All she saw was him.

"Yes." She whispered.

His mouth claimed hers, and his hand feathered down her stomach. She writhed under him. Her back arched, and she pushed against the palm of his hand where it cupped her, a finger sliding between her folds.

Kal played at her wet, ready entrance. A whimpier of need caught in her throat.

Oh, good God.

Slowly his finger pushed into her, methodically stroking her. She squirmed at the slow burn of pleasure. After a moment, he slipped in a second finger and started to work her, harder, faster. Her breath caught on a moan. Biting her lower lip, Maddie tried to stifle the cry of pleasure threatening to break free.

His fingers retreated and for a second a fear that he would stop shook her.

Instead, he leaned his head down and took one hard nipple into his mouth.

Maddie twined her fingers into his hair as he sucked her. A squeak of surprise escaped as he nibbled on the sensitive skin. Releasing the taut peak, he kissed the soft flesh. Maddie wrapped her legs around him, trying to keep him from leaving. She wasn't done.

Flicking the other nipple, she squeaked. She looked down into his eyes and nearly lost her mind at the mischief staring back.

A smile spread over his lips as he started to kiss a trail down her skin, over her stomach, down her belly, a hand wandering and teasing her, tickling the skin along her thigh.

Maddie squirmed. Crap, and she'd thought she was burning up before.

"Kal. I can't, please. I can't wait any longer."

His touch left a trail of release, but his mouth brought her closer and closer to desperation.

Finally, his lips found their destination. The heat of his tongue against her swollen clit had the pressure building in her so great she feared she'd burst to pieces.

"Kal."

He licked her again, his tongue stroking her. A blinding light behind her eyes blanked out the room. She raised her hand, unsure where to put it, unsure what to hold on to, unsure how to keep herself from grabbing him and mounting him.

As if Kal was in Maddie's head, he looked up from his quest, smirking from between her legs.

"You are impatient."

Her eyes widened, and she growled this time.

Kal answered the call, moving above her, altering his

position in one fluid motion. He held himself up above her, as he pushed up her leg to move between her legs. Looking down at him, at the angle of him, she couldn't stop the gasp.

How in the hell was he fitting in her?

Trying to catch air into her lungs, she barely got the words out. "Are you sure you're compatible with humans?"

God, she'd question the fact she believed in aliens later. Right now all she wanted was to be taken, mated, screwed, fucked, whatever he wanted to call it. She needed him.

Bracing herself, gripping his massive bicep, she waited for his answer.

"Very compatible, I promise you."

A feverish nod was all she could give.

A million years passed as he studied her. Cherished her. His gaze intense as he claimed her mouth. Gentle kisses at first, growing more fierce by the second. Maddie could feel the smooth skin of his dick against her entrance. Apprehension, anticipation, desire.

Rocking her hips, she pushed against him, his dick just out of reach.

Kal's hand reached down and held down her hips as he slowly pushed in.

The burning of muscles being stretched, a mix of sated need and new discomfort of unused muscles, she took him inch by inch. The pleasure of finally having him in her the only thing she cared about.

He pushed further in and Maddie tried meeting him, but he wouldn't let her move. Not yet.

His breath hissed out as he pulled away from her mouth.

The restraint evident in the lines of his face. "Yes, we are very compatable."

Her breath hitched the moment he pulled out and then thrust back in, quicker this time.

His pace still slow, methodical as he braced his body over her.

The desire within her coiled tighter and tighter.

Soon there was nothing but feeling, pleasure, need, desperation with each stroke.

"Maddie, you are mine," he whispered into her ear.

She closed her eyes, placing her hands around him, kneading his back.

"Yours."

In a fevered motion Kal took her faster and harder. Maddie moaned and cried out as he took her again and again. When she felt like she couldn't possibly take anymore, when her body began to pull from him, take from him, come for him, and yet he still needed more, she gave and gave until he began to quiver against her.

The word mine chanted on his breath and he lowered his head to her shoulder.

"You are mine." As he thrust in one last time, burning her to the very edge of all feeling, he spilled into her, as a sharp pain radiated from her shoulder.

In that moment, her energy, her magic mixed with his and a new magic she'd never felt before, took from her and took from him so much more than just a single moment of pleasure.

There was no catching her breath. She slowly dove into a state between sleep and lucidity as his warmth pulsed through her. This time the fire didn't burn. Instead, she welcomed it as he collapsed on her, rolling with her in his arms. He pulled her close. Her mind teetering close to sleep and a flood of images from somewhere she'd never been.

Dreams of a dragon soaring through the skies, feasting on the heat of the sun. Dreams of a life she'd never known, a planet far from here.

A heart beat through her that was not her own, the pulse comforting, protecting. Finally, sleep took hold with the knowledge of her warrior's love running through her veins. Her dragon, his soul, running through her veins.

Maddie's eyes flew open.

What had just happened? Running her hands over her body, Maddie realized she felt, well, normal.

Normal was good.

This was normal.

She sat up. Fuck, no it wasn't.

None of this was normal. She'd just met this guy like what, this morning?

Or wait, yesterday. It was dark, but somewhere in the early hours of morning. What time though? She shifted and blanched. Her muscles ached.

How many times had she and he made love? Three? Four? That last time she'd started it. Maddie couldn't get enough of him, even if every time she came she was sure she would sleep for days, and yet every time she simply wanted him more. Sliding her hand down her stomach, she questioned how the hell she already ached for him.

Reaching her hand out, she was met with empty sheets. She'd have worried, except she knew he was near and knew he was safe. The beating of his heart always somewhere within her subconscious told her he was here, near, and content.

Blinking into the darkness, Maddie loathed the cold in his absence. She waited for the pain, the fire to come back and it didn't. Relief.

"Kal?" she called into the dark. Nothing. Okay. He wasn't in the bathroom then.

Maddie didn't like the dark, never had. The dark of the desert even worse. She conjured up a small orb of light.

"Kal?"

Her skin lit up in the tattoos as she thought of him.

Well, that's handy.

Maybe the orb wasn't needed.

She swung her legs off the bed and stood up.

As she moved towards the door, his pulse grew stronger within her.

"Huh."

It's like sonar.

Glancing over her shoulder, she thought about turning back for clothing, and realized that Kal had seen her curves and loved them. This was a new confidence, and it was freeing.

Blowing out a breath, she stepped into the hall baring it all.

A smile crossed her lips as she remembered when they'd first met. Maddie thought he was being cocky. Maybe the chicken had been a little extreme, but he was indeed a god at something. The heat pooled between her legs again and she squeezed her thighs together. Maddie had to pause. Holy hell. She was going to come just from the memory.

Her hand darted out to the wall, holding herself up as she rode out the wave. How the hell was she supposed to function like this.

Breathing through it, she stood still for another moment.

Guess I'm not dead below the waist.

She giggled to herself. Rounding the corner into the kitchen, Maddie took in the house. She'd been notified that there was a house left to her when her mom had passed. Only, she hadn't wanted it. Staying here hadn't been any option. Not then.

Her mom had broken her heart. Why hadn't Maddie been enough to try and change her fate? Maybe now though, she couldn't understand it all, but she could understand that her mother had done what she thought was right. Like she always did. She always did what she thought was right. Just like calling Maddie back here, and for once it was exactly what Maddie hadn't known she needed.

Stepping into the living room, the glow of her tattoos reflected off of something in the corner.

She could still feel the pulse of Kal; he was safe, so she explored.

In the corner on a small table was a picture of Maddie and her mom. She picked it up, her thumb tracing the image. Mom had tried.

"Perhaps you could get dressed, dear."

Maddie jumped.

"Mother. Why are you here? Good God."

She dropped the frame and luckily caught it mid-fall with a freezing spell. Plucking it from the air, she set it back down.

"I wanted to tell you how proud I am. Of course, I thought you might have clothes on. Oh, wait, does our dragon have clothes on?"

Maddie slapped at the air where her mother was, straining her neck looking for him.

"Mother."

She laughed. "He wasn't your mate when we first saw him, so you can't blame me for admiring the scenery."

"But he is my mate now. You can't. Ugh. Just stay turned around in the corner. Can we have a heart-to-heart when I'm dressed?"

Her mother floated around the room. "Of course. Of course. Please stay safe, sweetheart. I'll be back soon."

Mom was such an odd duck. She knew she'd die in a house fire and hadn't sugar-coated things for Maddie. She'd also prepared Maddie for it for years. This house must have been part of the plan.

There was always a damn plan.

Maddie had left months before the fire. She'd broken all the ties she could. Anything to run away from the pain that was coming. Maddie had told herself she was leaving to get away from the fact that her mother wouldn't let her have any adventures or any mystery in her life, but it had been to try and run from the pain coming. Her mother had said there are some things you can't and shouldn't change.

That hadn't mattered though. She had wanted to change something. She had wanted guarantees that her mother would come back as a ghost even if she died. She had wanted guarantees in life that she could change things. Ghost hunting had shed light on some things, but it never filled the void her mother's hugs left.

In the end, it had been a fire started by a strike of lightening that kill her. How odd that fire was now Maddie's friend.

Strange how life worked.

Maddie held out her palm and went to cast a fire spell. Instead, the fire appeared as she thought of it. The little flame danced on her hand.

Studying the little wick, she truly didn't understand.

Best she find Kal.

Listening into the night, his voice filtered in from out back.

"Perhaps we should bring them back to the ship as quickly as we can?"

Listening, there were no other voices.

Stepping into the backyard it took a minute before she found his shadow in the corner.

The small patch of grass tickled her feet before they reached cold stone. When was the last time she'd gone outside barefoot? Is this what freedom felt like?

When was the last time she'd gone outside naked? Never. That was a big never. Well, she could cross that off the list of things to do before you die.

Kal nodded as Maddie reached out to him. He took her into his embrace, pulling her in, and she allowed him.

Of course, she allowed him. This was home. Wherever he was; was home. It took a minute to realize the familiar ache in her heart, the one that never seemed to ever really go away, had finally quieted.

"Yeah. Sorry, Eadric. I'm fine. You'll like her, promise. Okay. Report later."

Snuggling against his shirtless torso, it occurred to her, he didn't seem to hang up anything.

"Who were you talking to?"

The light of the moon cast a glow around him as he looked down to her.

"My brothers. I'd ignored their calling all day. Eadric had reported I'd been turned into a bird."

She kissed the skin of his chest.

"Yeah. Sorry about that. I wasn't looking for anyone, and I

really hate settling down. It wasn't a good time. The bird might have been a little extreme."

"A chicken." He shook his head.

"Well. You walked into the Drunken Rooster. It was the first thing that came to mind."

His chest vibrated with laughter. "Too bad for me I didn't walk into somewhere more manly then."

His hand slipped below her chin and forced her to meet his eyes. "I hope that things have changed? Your view on love and perhaps this idea of settling down?"

Opening her mouth, she closed it again. Love. What exactly was this? Flashing back to her lust drunk-high on magic state didn't help. She'd said she was his. And she'd meant that. But love? What exactly was love?

He kissed her forehead, then her cheek.

"I see, mate, that you have not replaced your clothing."

He bent to kiss her.

Maddie's hands found their way up the muscles of his stomach.

She giggled as he reached around and grabbed her ass, lifting her up.

He pulled her against him, his cock pressing against the pants he'd put on.

She reached between them and stroked through the fabric. "Already?"

He smiled. "I am always ready for my mate."

8

*T*he smell of something delicious woke him from the world's worst dream. If he ever pissed off Maddie again, goddess help him. He never wanted to feel powerless like that again.

Stretching, his hand searched for her. Maddie was gone. His dragon sniffed at the air, and realizing there was no reason to panic, went back to relaxing.

Kal smiled. She wasn't far and after last night and this morning and all the other times she wasn't going to leave.

He knew that sating his mate would take a few hundred years, but no one had mentioned it also meant that it would take a lot of willpower to keep her off of him.

He liked it.

What he didn't like was waking without her in his arms.

Scanning the room, he grumbled. For fuck's sake, where were his pants? He needed to talk to her. Perhaps clothing was a good first step.

His stomach growled. Sex didn't feed a dragon, although it did make for a very docile one.

Kal rubbed at his chest. He needed to go flying soon. Being caged didn't make them happy, but at least the mate helped.

Lifting up the pants he'd finally found, his COM bounced as it hit the floor. He grabbed at it and put it away.

There wasn't a real need for the device, except backup. They could all talk by telepathy, and yet in human form they still relied on mechanical devices. Whatever. He couldn't wait to get back home where everything made sense. Their magic wasn't predictable here. He was only relieved that Maddie appeared to be fine, finally.

Now, mission one was to find his mate, and then food. Then back to the ship.

Peeking down the hall, he followed the sounds of clanging and banging. Kal could pick out Maddie in a crowd, but add her scent to whatever she was cooking and his stomach wasn't the only thing waking up.

"What is that delicious smell?" he asked, coming up behind her. Wrapping her in his arms, Kal breathed her in.

She relaxed into him, a perfect fit. Their soul, his dragon, they were going to be okay. This had been what he needed. He was too young to be abstinent too, but moreover he was too young to lose himself to the power. He rubbed up against her backside and hoped she'd get the hint.

"Kal? That better not be what I think it is."

He smiled. "What do you think it is?"

She dropped the spatula on the stove and turned in his arms.

"Well, I've established you don't seem to own a gun or any other weapon. So…"

He liked this little witch.

"Maddie? How are you feeling today?"

She shrugged. "You mean other than being sore in places I didn't know existed? Yeah, actually. I think I'm good."

Kal placed a hand against her cheek and her forehead. Her temperature seemed to be relatively normal. Her skin contained a glow that he found beautiful and pretty much what came with the territory of being his mate.

"Well, there is one thing, Kal, this."

He watched her hold up her hand as a tiny flame appeared. He shrugged.

"Is that not normal?" he asked. "Fire is very normal for a dragon."

She pursed her lips. "Only, I'm not a dragon and I didn't conjure it."

Kal lifted her hand and kissed it through the flame.

"Kal!"

He pulled away.

"You are a dragon's mate. You share some of my powers. You can't transform, but you will be able to communicate with me through your mind." He leaned in and kissed her temple. "You will be able to control fire and it will never hurt you." He slipped a finger over the flame. "You are nearly immortal."

Kal took her hand and rested it over his heart. "You are my heart. As long as my heart beats my life is yours."

He couldn't make out her thoughts yet. Not really. That would come though.

Maddie pinched her lips closed. She was indeed thinking, that couldn't be good.

"Mate? What has you silent now?"

Kal liked the way she looked up at him. Reaching for her, he tried to pull her in, but she pushed away.

This was not how he saw his morning going, which had

his dragon chuckling. This was exactly how they'd seen finding a mate happening, though minus the chicken.

"Right. So that's my question. You bite me and I'm now your mate?"

He nodded, his senses on edge. Where was she going with this now?

"So my wedding present is this scar, some tattoos, and fire?"

Kal didn't think he was exceptionally good at reading females anymore, but he could definitely see the warning bells going off. Okay. He'd bite.

"Wedding present?" Kal asked.

Maddie's nose wrinkled as if something had just spoiled and was smelling up the kitchen.

He wasn't sure if he should apologize right now or wait until he actually understood what had just happened.

"Great. This is my life. I don't get a wedding. I get screwed, both literally and figuratively."

Her face reddened, and he didn't have to ask what she meant as the air scented of her. He ran a hand down her back to her hip. He was dying to get under the shirt she wore, but as clouds rolled into her eyes he dropped his hands and surrendered.

"Maddie, if I have done something wrong, please let me know. In our culture we would have feasts and celebrations. We will, when we return home. The warriors are highly revered, and finding our mates is something to be celebrated. But not here."

Her shoulders relaxed, and she rested her hand on his forearm.

"I asked for your permission, I assumed you understood what I meant. On this planet everything is wrong. I don't know all your customs, and I assumed that you felt what I felt."

Her fingers twisted on the hair along his arm, the only sound a popping on the stove. She quickly spun around and turned a knob, coming right back to him.

"No. I understood what you wanted to do," Maddie said.

She stopped scowling, but he wasn't any less confused.

"I suppose I just want what any little girl wants. To be the center of attention."

Center of attention, he understood.

"You are the center of my world, mate." Bending down, he gently took her lips with a soft kiss.

"I understand. But-" Maddie let out an audible sigh.

"But what?" Kal was back to feeling like maybe he wasn't enough. Why did he have to learn the feeling of doubt now? Or ever. He didn't need this useless feeling.

"But, now that I found someone that..." she stopped.

Good, Lord. That what? Was this a guessing game? He really sucked at humanity. He needed the whole telepatic communication to start kicking in at any minute.

"Well, it's just that I finally found someone worth walking down the aisle for. Someone worth celebrating. I've never wanted attention, but right now I can see that whole dream that everyone says you see when you find the right one."

Kal followed her movements as she swayed one side then the other, then she lifted a finger and brought it to rest on his stomach. He liked where this might be going, if it was going anywhere near his dick, anyway. This woman had him ready to do as she wished. Wherever she wished.

"Well, I suppose I don't really mind not getting a wedding. I had that chance once and didn't want it."

Kal started and his dragon awoke at her words. They glared at her.

"Wedding?"

Maddie seemed to bite back a smile. His eyes narrowed in irritation.

"Yeah. That's sort of what humans do to mate another human, Kal. I suppose shifters have mating rituals, the Fae do some really weird shit. But humans have a wedding."

Kal grabbed her wrist, pulling her against him.

His dragon did not like the idea of anyone coming near their mate. His dick grew harder with a need to mark her again. Fill her, sate her, and remind her just who she was now.

"What?" she asked, obviously feeling the mood change.

Jealousy consumed him. Another useless human emotion he didn't like.

"This other mate, this human. You almost let him mark you?"

He pulled her in closer, grabbing her ass. No room for escape, his dick resting on her stomach.

"Oh!" She said in surprise.

"Answer me. Did you?"

Her smile fell, but the air scented of her arousal.

"I. Well, it's not marking. Not really. It's called marriage. The only sign of mating, as you call it, is a ring. But, people get divorced all the time."

Kal slipped his fingers under her nightgown, tracing the line of her panties.

"What is divorce?"

She swallowed.

"It's when a marriage is ended. But, people re-marry too. I don't see why this is an issue."

Lifting the edge of her panties, he slid his fingers underneath, following the line down her ass to the crease of her thigh.

"Was the human the coward at the bar?"

Her breathing changed. He listened to her heart beat speed up.

"I. Uh. Yes."

He growled.

"He would never have made you happy. You are not his."

She nodded.

"We do not end. You are mine, forever," Kal finished.

The flush of her cheeks was all he needed as encouragement to push forward his fingers going further south.

"Forever?" she said, her voice husky.

Sliding two fingers between her folds, he entered her. Maddie's eyes closed as he stroked her slowly at first.

"Forever."

She moaned with each thrust.

"You are mine." He leaned in, close enough to whisper in her ear. "Say it."

She sucked in air as he worked her. "Yours."

"Very good."

Kal kissed her, swallowing her next whimper of pleasure.

"Turn around."

Her breathing heavy, she didn't question him as his fingers retreated. She turned as he unsnapped his pants.

Sliding his hand around her neck, down her back to the edge of her nightgown, he gripped the hem and reached below, pushing aside her panties. His fingers passed over her heat once more, but this time only to tease.

She was slick and ready. This was good, because this time there was no foreplay. This time it was all animal. All to erase whoever she'd once thought she would belong to. He wanted to take her, own her, make her know who her mate was.

Holding her panties aside, he positioned the tip of his dick at her entrance, bending her over the counter. Without warning he pushed in, sliding past the protest of her tight muscles. He pushed in, slowly at first, letting her accept him once again.

This time it was his turn to bite back a groan of pleasure.

Her whimpers and cries of need music to his ears, knowing he was the one she was thinking about. He was the one making her come. He was the one filling her over and over.

"You. Are. Mine."

Kal waited, waited to feel her muscles pulling from him, desperate for him to finish her. He waited for her to beg him to finish her.

"Kal. Please. Kal."

Her body began to quake around him and that was all his dick needed as encouragement.

Kal lifted her leg allowing him in deeper. He pushed in once, twice, three times, and she screamed out.

Now. Now he would allow himself. Now that she was his. Now that her body was begging. He thrust one last time. Spilling into her. Proving to her that he would only ever be the one for her.

Kal kissed Maddie's shoulder as he watched her sleep. She wouldn't wake for some time, that he could be sure of. Perhaps he should be more gentle with his new mate. Kal chuckled. No. She'd enjoyed it. Her body needed it. He needed her.

His dragon curled up in his soul as he drew comfort from her sleeping form.

Our mate.

Fate had smiled favorably on him. Her curves were delicious and Kal couldn't look away from his mate's beauty.

She brought a peace foreign and desperately needed. His soul finally rested rather than reaching a near destructive state. The price of giving himself to her was his soul's stability. Maybe that would make him a better warrior.

He hadn't been thrilled about this mission. In Kal's mind his planet went through extreme lengths to ensure the survival of the warriors. His brothers hadn't truly understood any better than he had. But, now, in this moment he understood.

He kissed her again. "Dream, my love."

There was no resisting her. Kal ran a hand the length of her body, over her hips, over her amazing ass. He grew hard just thinking of what he could do to her, the millions of places they hadn't christened.

When he got her back to his home, he was allowed as much time as he needed to mate her. Once she was settled, and pregnant, then he'd go back to active duty, but his sole purpose for the foreseeable future was to explore her. Know her. Love her.

The future seemed bright, finally. A weight lifted from him, one that he hadn't realized. It had almost seemed too much to keep the warriors viable. Save the universe or the galaxy, fine. But to keep his species going? Too much. Finding her was as if the sun had only ever been shining with half its strength until now.

Kal cringed as a subtle beeping shattered his peace.

Fuck. What now?

It wasn't like Kal didn't know. It was a signal from the ship.

He opened up his mind and listened. Deo was most likely shouting to any of them that weren't there yet.

You need to meet back here, brother. 24-hours. That was the rule.

Curling his lip, he was right as the harsh voice broke the serenity. Apparently his brother hadn't found his mate yet, or maybe he wouldn't be so damn uptight.

Deo, move the ship and ping me with coordinates. I found her and will bring her back soon.

He could practically hear Deo's grunt.

No. We need to meet as a group. Nyke's found trouble.

Kal sat up, the blanket falling to the bed. Of course he had. He'd missed out on a sense of humor the day the goddess handed that bit of personality out.

Alright. I'll be there soon.

Kal tried to shut off the communications going back and forth between the others.

They'd at least tried to leave him alone.

"Maddie?"

He leaned over and kissed the skin of her shoulder.

She moaned and rolled over, her breasts exposed and begging to be tasted.

Well, fuck.

No. He had to have some kind of self restraint. But, fuck me. Why?

He circled a nipple, the nub peaking at his touch. Kal studied her face as her eyes fluttered open.

"Is it morning? Or afternoon?"

His hand overflowed with her as he cupped her breast. Goddess, he loved this woman.

"Afternoon, I believe. Your days are so short that I find myself very confused often."

She stretched, the sheet further flowing down her body.

Son of a bitch.

He wanted her and instead of taking her,he had to go to some fucking meeting of the minds. Fuck those fuckers. Only, the warrior within knew you didn't ignore your brothers. If one was in need, if one was worried, if one was happy, you joined in.

"I need to go," he said.

Maddie's eyes flew open, and she sat up.

"What?"

He chuckled. "Not forever. I need to go meet my brothers."

A foreign tension struck him. It settled, and he realized it was hers. Good. They were connected. Taking her hand within his own, he felt her unravel a bit.

"Oh, okay. You'll be back?"

He nodded.

"Brothers? How many of you are there?"

The damn temptress made thinking very difficult as his eyes were drawn back to her naked breasts.

"Here? Or overall?"

His mouth watered.

He watched as her lips puckered in thought. He'd kiss those sexy lips before he left. Kal was making his next mission to ensure she did nothing else but think of him until he returned.

"Here, I guess? Was that other guy one of them? The one I scared off when you, or well I, turned you into a chicken?"

He rolled his eyes. That was a shitty memory.

"Yes. That was one of them."

Pulling her knees up, she got comfortable.

"Are you all so, so, uh, huge?"

His eyes narrowed.

"I don't think I like what you're insinuating. I am enough for you, mate. You do not need anyone else."

Maddie let out a loud musical laugh. He liked the sound, but it confused him.

"You are a fool for being such a cocky ass."

He righted himself on the bed. "I'm sorry?"

Rising on her knees, she came to him.

"I just wanted to know if you were all dragons and if you were all muscle-heads. You stick out like a weed around here. We may need to help them blend in a bit more. Help them figure out how to talk with women. No one else needs to be a chicken, do they?"

Kal shuddered.

Maddie wrapped her arms around his neck as she raised her face to meet his.

"Oh. Perhaps you might help. But, not right now. Right now, I want you to sleep. Be ready for me when I come back. Your only job today is to lay here and ready yourself for when I return. You will not be getting much sleep tonight or for the foreseeable future."

He liked the stutter of her breath as he wrapped his arms around her.

"I see. And how, the hell, should I ready myself?"

Maddie pulled away, enough to slip a hand between them. His eyes followed her as she ran the palm down her breasts, her stomach, down, down, slipping her own fingers between the vee of her thighs.

Well, fuck. Fuck. Fuck. Fuck.

"Maddie. You're killing me."

Licking her lips, she smiled. "Am I? Because to me, you

look to be quite alive." Her eyes flicked down to his erect dick.

"Woman. You need to tame yourself or I won't be able to leave and that would be very, very unforgivable."

"Fine," she said, as her hands flew up in the air. "At least I tried."

He got out of bed slowly. Good goddess, he needed his dick to settle down.

Grabbing up his pants, he slid them on and stood there.

Well, shit.

Maddie's laughter had him scowling.

"Do you have a problem there big boy?"

He stood, hands on hips.

"This is your doing, mate."

The vision of her crawling towards him nearly had him bursting.

"Maddie. What are you playing at?"

Kal didn't like the look on her face. Trouble.

"I'm just coming to help you. It looks like that guy," she pointed to his erection, "isn't going to fit into those tight pants."

He cocked his head. "And, what exactly are you going to do to help that?"

He didn't wait long before the warmth of her mouth slid down the shaft and his eyes nearly rolled back into his skull.

What the fuck was he supposed to do? You don't say no to your mate.

His brothers could wait a bit longer. Long enough for him to fit back into his pants, anyway. He'd be quick. Her tongue did something that he'd fucking dream about for the rest of his life. Yeah. He'd be fast. Those assholes better have news worthy of him having to leave her.

9

*M*addie downed a drink while Kal scowled.

Her dragon wasn't enjoying himself, well, tough. Kal had given in to going out. Of course he had. Kal returned in a pissed off mood, ranting that they needed to leave immediately.

She'd waited for the panic to hit. The idea that she'd be leaving not only this crappy town, but earth. Right. Insane. It was insane, but the dreams of Kal's home told her she wasn't crazy.

She was more than happy to leave this town, but this time she wanted to do it right.

"Come on, Kal. It's my last day on earth."

He scowled further.

"Those men have been watching you all night."

Maddie shrugged.

"And those women have been checking you out all night."

"I don't care." If looks could kill, someone would have been dead by now.

She smiled. Kal wasn't going to ruin this. She had one re-do. One chance to leave everything the way she should have.

"Really? Kal, you don't care about all of these girls, like literally all these girls in this whole place are checking you out."

He closed the inches between them.

"I have a mate. I don't need any of them. What I do not like is someone looking at what is mine."

Maddie craned her head around, because seriously, who in the hell would want her? Besides the insane and incredible sexy dragon-alien-man holding her, which was still a mystery.

"Kal. You need to chill. Let's go have fun."

Maddie let the beat of the odd Fae music pull her into the trance, the dance floor full of people. As they reached the edge of the crowded space, Kal paused.

"Kal, come on. If I have to go with you somewhere, you can at least help me have no regrets leaving." Maddie sputtered in laughter as she looked up. His eyes wide as saucers, and his normally tanned skin, white.

"It's just dancing," she yelled over the music.

"I don't do this kind of dancing."

Kal looked over her head and back down at her. "How is this acceptable in front of others? Mating is a very private thing to my kind."

Maddie laughed. "They aren't mating." She stopped and took in the crowd. "Probably."

Shaking his head, he tried to pull her away from the crowd.

"Kal, come on. I want to dance."

Someone came up behind her, hugging her in a drunk-girl grip. "Maddie. Come on. Let's dance. Grab your boyfriend, I'll take his back."

Kal blanched. "She isn't taking my anything."

Pinching her eyes closed, Maddie breathed through the laughter.

"It's fine. She just meant she'd, never mind."

Maddie watched Kal glance from her to the crowd to Ellen. Oh, this should be good. She couldn't exactly hear his thoughts, and she was thinking that right now maybe, it was a good thing. Maddie could still use what was coming next.

"I'll stand here and watch you."

Yup. That was pretty close.

"Okay. Because that's less creepy, Kal."

If he wasn't so damn hot, maybe this would bug her more. For now though, she'd keep him around.

Ellen grabbed Maddie's hand and started to walk.

"Let's go. I need to get my dance on!"

A second glance back at Kal's scowl. One chance, this was her one chance. She shrugged and went. He'd be fine. Or well, he should be fine. He could take care of himself. Tonight was for her. Her last night. Tomorrow they'd leave to find the mates of the others and then off to wherever home would be.

Ellen led her out into the throng of people. She slid through a couple grinding. Pushing her too-wide hips through this crowd was a pain. Maddie had never felt sexy in her life, not until she'd met Kal. Until she could feel the beat of Kal's heart when he looked at her.

Raising her arms, she started to sway with the rhythm.

"I knew this place would be a trip," Ellen shouted.

Maddie smiled.

She felt sexy and confident. Hopefully Kal could see her dancing.

Closing her eyes, the music flowed through her. She wouldn't miss Roswell. She never really did. She just missed her mom. Maddie pushed that away. Her mom would find her before she left. She knew she would.

A humming flowed through her body, radiating from her stomach. In the back of her mind she figured that was probably the drinks, the Fae always did things like that. She didn't care. Peace wasn't something she'd felt, ever.

The rhythm of the music pulled her. Maddie's body flowed in movement to the trance. Letting all the stress of the day, her week, her life be taken away with whatever magic laced this place.

In her own world, she liked herself. She liked her newfound confidence in life. She liked that for the first time she didn't mind knowing her future, or at least who her future would be with.

The beat changed slower. Her cares seemed to float away.

Someone came up behind her. Her mind wouldn't work the way it should. She should have known to stay away from the drinks here. She just didn't or perhaps hadn't cared.

Alarm tried to push through the fog. It wasn't Kal. She knew that. Maddie could feel the beat of his heart, could tell where he was without thinking. Kal was here, close, and this wasn't him. Opening her eyes she blinked, nothing cleared, she still felt underwater and everything muted. Worry, concern, life, a dull matter.

The heat of the person behind her was too close though. Panic should have kicked in by now, but she'd have to push through the murky swamp of the Fae magic, and that just wasn't happening.

Maddie followed Ellen's lead and danced without care. Then an unwelcome hand rested on her hip.

"Hey beautiful."

Maddie, still magic drunk, funneled her newfound power to her fingertips and burned his hand.

He squealed.

"Ah. Shit, Maddie. It's me."

Everything seemed so slow as she turned.

"Donnie?"

He smiled.

"Yeah. You look amazing. I've never seen you wear a skirt like this before."

Maddie thought she'd stopped dancing, but the room still swayed.

"Yeah. It's like a new confidence thing."

Her hands smoothed down the skirt she'd borrowed from Ellen as she tilted. Thankfully, or unthankfully, Donnie stopped her from falling.

"Careful."

Ellen's head swam. The skirt. Right. The skirt she liked. Donnie? Ex, she didn't. But the skirt, right? Kal. Kal had liked it. And if Kal liked it. Maddie liked to be in it. Hell, if Maddie liked it she was going to start fucking wearing it from now on. Kal. Right. Where was Kal?

"I like this new you. So you are back for real?" Donnie's voice broke the fog.

Why was his voice getting through to her? Fae, he was part something she thought she remembered.

His hand reached out to pull her close. Maddie tried to pull away.

"Don't,Donnie."

He scowled.

"Why not? I'm glad to see you ditched that weight lifter dude. He was so wrong for you."

World swimming again. Man, she hated Fae magic. This wasn't working for her.

"And why is he wrong for me? Because he was good looking? Because he wants me?"

Oh, crap. She started to feel dizzy. Breathing, she regrouped. What had she been doing?

Oh right. Kal. "Because the sex is the best damn sex I've ever had?"

Donnie's lip curled and his eyes narrowed.

"You slept with him? Fuck, Maddie. What the hell. Whatever. It's fine. It's not like we're together again or anything. Not yet."

He reached for her again and she attempted to pull away. The world moved a lot slower than she remembered.

Kal. All she could do was think of Kal. As Donnie got too close, Kal's massive hand reached from behind her, grabbing his forearm and stopping him.

She blinked at the spinning.

Oh, good. The only words going through her head.

Kal growled, a muted but familiar sound in her foggy haze.

"She has already told you no," Kal growled.

Maddie tried to smile, pity wasn't really her thing though.

"Donnie, Kal. Kal, this is Donnie."

Donnie grabbed his arm back.

"Don't you dare touch me, you freak." Donnie's eyes grew wide. "What the hell are your tattoos doing?"

Maddie glanced at her arms and shrugged.

"Glowing."

Donnie glanced back at Kal, Maddie following his glare.

"What the fuck. Why do his glow too?"

Maddie would not get to break it to Donnie softly. There was no way to soften anything, and she didn't owe him anything. Not anymore. She'd done everything she could, except marry him just because he believed he loved her.

"She's my mate. You will keep your hands off of her," Kal said.

Kal ran a hand down her bare arm, sending shivers up her spine.

"Mate?" Donnie's voice screamed over the crowd. Maddie half expected everyone to stop and turn to look at them.

Maddie's movements were slightly slower than normal as she reached up and laid her palm against Kal's cheek. Reassuring him and reassuring herself, she supposed.

"Yes, Donnie. Wife, mate. Same thing really. But yes," she shouted over the crowd. Somehow it didn't seem as loud now though. Wow. These were some good drinks.

A rumble vibrated through Kal's chest, waking her a bit.

"No. Mate. Wife is not for an eternity, a mate cannot leave, ever. We are soul bound."

Donnie's face turned a few different shades of scarlet.

Sort of pretty, Maddie thought.

"Maddie, don't do this. You don't understand. These guys, they are bad news."

Kal's arm encircled her and she smiled. He was the only kind of trouble she'd ever need.

"I might not know everything, but I promise you, Donnie, I'm safe."

In her relaxed state she tried to reach out to Kal with her mind.

I think I'm ready to go.

His arm squeezed tighter.

I thought you'd never ask.

Kal pulled her away and dragged her in front of him.

"Wait!" Donnie called.

They didn't.

Maddie passed Ellen who was making out with her husband. At some point in life Maddie had thought wolf shifters hot. If she'd only known.

Maddie wished Ellen all the happiness in the world.

She smiled to herself. She felt happy. This was happy. Crap, she was Fae drunk.

Nudging her, Maddie followed with Kal to continue past and towards the door. She smiled to herself, it was nice to see that anyone she'd be leaving behind would be fine. Except Donnie. But right now, that might not be something she could control.

Maddie could see the door in front of her, so close. The strobe lights behind them and less hypnotic, her head seemed to clear a little. Kal grabbed up her hand, the warmth of their connection flowing through her. Yup, she was good with this.

As they walked past the bouncer out onto the street, Maddie snuggled into Kal.

"Mate. I know what you are thinking."

She smiled. "Kal, I highly doubt that."

He stroked her back. "You may not be able to connect with me well yet, but I can still feel your emotions."

She shrugged. Secrets weren't healthy for a relationship, anyway.

"Fine then. Tell me. What am I thinking?"

They stopped.

"Aside from the fact you smell like sex, you also smell of longing. You aren't happy with leaving that human behind, are you?"

Maddie swallowed. That really wasn't right, but he nailed the longing part. She just wasn't sure what it really was. Her mom mostly.

"I don't regret leaving him. I do wish that maybe things would have been different. I wish he was different and not still waiting for me. But, mostly I just want to say goodbye to my mom. We wouldn't leave without her, right? I mean without saying goodbye?"

"We will wait as long as needed, my love, my mate. The benefit of being a dragon is I can fly wherever my brothers might wander off to. We are stronger together, but they would understand."

She nodded. What was her problem really? A moment ago she was happy and carefree and now, well not so much.

"Let's just walk home. Thanks for coming out with me." Maddie started to tip over. All right, not quite sober, but at least the Fae magic wasn't still clouding her judgement.

Moving forward, she leaned against Kal. The heat of the day still lingered on the concrete, while the air cooled more rapidly. The flashes of images from Kal's planet surfaced.

"Kal? What's your home like?"

She leaned closer.

"Our home, you mean."

He put a hand on her shoulder.

"Are you cold, my love?"

Maddie nodded.

"Yes. And yes. Our home."

Heat radiated out from Kal's hand, filling her and covering her body.

"Better?"

She was better. She could get used to his strange magic.

"Our home. It's beautiful. Different, and the air is thicker with magic. Earth doesn't come close to the amount of magic we have. It's warmer too. Much warmer."

Kal paused.

"Maddie? Can you protect yourself? I mean, other than turn me into a chicken?"

She nodded. Tapping into their shared connection, she tried to feel what he felt. Anger. Fear. Protective.

"We're being followed. Whatever you can do, do it."

Allowing Kal to push her along, they ducked into an alley and waited in the shadows.

Three figures came to the mouth.

"We know what you are, alien."

Kal stepped out, Maddie tried to grip his shirt to pull him back, but there was no controlling him.

She wrinkled her nose at the stench of the nearby dumpster as her own fear started to unravel within her. Clutching her hands to her stomach, she watched. Remaining hidden, she tried to cast a protection spell, something that wasn't entirely her thing.

"I don't think you have any idea what I am. Who are you?" Kal asked.

"Give us back the girl and we won't hurt you."

Kal grunted. "I won't give her back. And I don't think you will hurt me."

The three figures moved back.

"If you hurt us, I guarantee you'll make everything much worse. Tell us where you're from."

Kal didn't turn to Maddie; he started walking forward.

"How about you leave that being my business and you will all live to see tomorrow. I'll be gone soon enough and it will no longer be your problem."

Maddie couldn't make out the third body. He or she kept just out of sight around the side of the building. She definitely didn't recognize the others.

Silence followed. A few cars went down the street, but there wasn't much going on downtown on a weeknight.

"Kal?" she whispered.

In her head she could hear him.

Stay hidden. I'll be right back.

Maddie faded into the background as close to the wall as possible.

Something whizzed through the air past Kal.

What was that?

She hoped he heard her.

"Shooting darts at me isn't a good choice."

A feminine voice called back, "then don't give us reason. Return the human and tell us where you're from. Our boss can be very generous."

Another whizzing. Kal roared, and he took off toward the entrance.

"I told you not to do that."

Maddie could see his shift starting as he breathed a wall of fire out in front of him. All she could see was the scattering of three bodies.

A second later Kal's dragon form came up to her. She stared into his eye, large, orange, with large slits for pupils. Scary, if she didn't know it was Kal.

Get on.

Maddie looked at his extended leg and stepped up. She jumped to get atop his neck and squealed as her skirt rode up. God, if they weren't being attacked this would be embarrassing.

Maddie looked around at the small space where Kal nearly touched both walls. How the hell were they getting out of this?

Hang on. Kal's voice filled her head.

She studied his neck and had no idea what the hell to hang on to.

Maddie conjured up a bit of rope around his neck just as he jumped and sunk his massive claws into the wall of the building.

Clenching her thighs around him, she held on. Crumbles of stone clanked to the ground as they climbed.

Great. She'd have to come back and magic that shit away tomorrow.

They climbed up and onto the roof.

The building wasn't that tall, and it took only a second. Kal probably could have jumped had he had more space. Once on the roof, he pushed up, meeting the sky and took off into the night.

"Who were they?"

The dragon grunted. Apparently he didn't know, making being chased more scary. They knew about him, but he didn't know them. He didn't know he was being hunted.

*I*f she stayed here much longer, Maddie would have to paint the ceiling. Her nerves wouldn't let her sleep, so instead she stared up at the blank white canvas.

Who the hell were those guys last night? Something had seemed familiar, but she couldn't put her finger on it. Her magic etched the scene over and over in the air, but she finally stopped obsessing and let the images fade. This wasn't helping. Her mother would be helpful right now.

Things hadn't been the same last night. Kal had been protective, cautious. He was almost afraid this morning when he needed to go find his brothers. Maddie had wanted to go with him, but he'd felt she would be safer here. Or at least safer away from him and his brothers.

Stretching, she kicked off the covers. It was no use. She couldn't go back to sleep.

Sitting up, Maddie moved slowly. Her body was sore from all the working out she'd done with Kal. Maybe she'd bother finding a scale and see if she'd lost any weight. Maybe on her new planet the gravity would be less and she'd weigh less there. So many hopes.

Rolling her eyes, she laughed. She could deal with going to another planet, why not? But, Maddie still hadn't wrapped her head around being mates, married, never alone again. This was the best time of her life. What would it be like to wake up to him every day? Was this all a dream? Maybe she'd hit her head, and this was all made up.

The images though. Everything felt so real. The dream of his planet, they weren't hers. But they too were real. She knew it all was real.

What should she do to kill time? Not leave. Kal had been insistent. Fine. She'd listen. It wasn't like she hadn't seen horror movies before. Or read books where the heroine did something dumb and got herself kidnapped. No. She'd just stay. Fine. But, lordy. Mundane. Without him everything was meaningless.

Padding down to the kitchen, her stomach growled in a reminder of how hungry she was. Daydreaming, she grabbed up some bread. She'd miss bread, or at least Earth bread. Finding some peanut butter and jelly she made what she hoped wouldn't be the last sandwich she ever had.

Spreading the knife over the soft surface, she smiled. Her mother's annoying talents finally paid off. This house was exactly what Maddie needed, for now anyway. Maybe the rest of Kal's brothers would come knocking. Maybe they wouldn't. She had no idea what being mates meant for the rest of his warriors, pack, no -warriors. Whatever.

Maddie somehow knew them though. Images of their planet, of each one of them, all there. Was this part of mating? Maybe she'd siphoned his memories along with his powers?

No. This seemed like something he would have wanted to share.

Holding out her hand, she let flames slide through each finger. This was just weird. Holding a finger to the bread, she watched as it browned. That was handy.

This was her new life. The knowledge that floated around in her head.

When he wasn't making her body come at the snap of his fingers, he made her mind curious and wonder. He made her laugh. He was her peace.

Another planet. Sure, why not? There wasn't much here for her, anyway.

Maddie swallowed. Another planet. Okay. That sounded a little more strange, a little less like a vacation and more like she'd lost her mind.

Swallowing down the dry bite, she doubted herself again. What if she was dreaming this all up? Witches, shifters, vampires, goblins, freaky Fae people. Aliens? Uh. That one had her mind stretched a little thin.

"Mom?"

The room temperature droped a few degrees as her mother shimmered into existence.

Sure, now the woman came when called.

"Yes, dear?"

Maddie rubbed her temples.

"Mom? This whole Kal thing. He's real, right?"

Her mother's ghost shimmered in and out as she milled about.

"Oh yes, dear. I'm pretty sure your body can tell he's real."

Maddie's face heated. "Yeah. Okay. Right. But what about this whole space thing?"

Her mother paused. "Oh that. Yes, yes. Of course. He's really not from here."

Rolling her eyes, she stood. "Mom. I get he isn't from here, but what does that mean?"

Her mom started to bob again and shimmer in and out before stopping.

"I mean, Maddie, sweetheart. He's from another world. One much more complex than even our own. You'll live for an eternity there, or well, much longer than your mind can grasp. Their magic is so much more than even yours."

Right. Okay.

It's real. She'd be leaving. From the corner of her eye, Maddie caught her mother's ghost going from corner to corner, crossing the room, circling back.

"Mother? What's going on? Please settle down. I won't leave if you don't want me to."

Her chest tightened.

Okay. Maybe she'd have to come up with another solution.

"No. No. Dear, you have to go. It's uh. Well; promise me you'll do as I say and he will come for you."

Tilting her head, she glared at her mom. "I'd ask if you were drunk, but I know that's not a ghost thing."

She suddenly noticed her mother wringing her hands.

"Mom? Are you okay? You're a ghost. You shouldn't be stressed out."

Maddie's mom stopped in front of her, taking on a mostly corporeal figure.

"Sweetie. You don't understand. Kal is meant to be yours, but with him comes one more hurdle. One that I have tried to see any other way around. There is none. If all goes as planned, you will come out stronger. If all does not go as planned, well, we best never think that way. In all the variations of the future, Kal has never failed."

Maddie's heart pounded to the beat of sheer panic.

"Mother, now you're just scaring me."

Her mother nodded. "Yes. Okay. Good. That means you'll listen."

Maddie reached for her mother's hands. They weren't quite human, but as she let her magic flow, her mother appeared more and more alive. Perhaps whatever it was wouldn't be too bad, and if it was, at least she got to hold her mother's hands one more time.

"When they come for you, don't use your magic. Or well, attempt to not use it much."

"Mother? Who is 'they'?"

Her mom nibbled her lip. "You'll find out soon enough." Her eyes darted to the door.

"Madeleine? Forgive me, but this is for your own good. And, just remember he will come for you. It's best these people don't know your true powers."

Maddie tried to pull her hands away from her mother, her words scaring her. What the hell. She couldn't pull away as if her hands were somehow glued to her mother's in an electric current. Within a few seconds Maddie suddenly felt drained and stumbled backwards.

"Mother? What did you do?"

Trying to raise an arm, she grunted in the effort. Maddie didn't even have the energy to be scared anymore.

Her mother's face blurred in and out of focus.

"Oh, I'm so sorry. This is the best way to protect you. Your magic will return to full strength soon enough. I had Mrs. Webber cast a transfer spell for me. You know how weak she is though, but I needed to. They are of little threat to you being weak. You will need to protect Kal and his brothers, and you will. But right now, you need to protect you, first."

"Who is 'they'." Sinking to the floor, Maddie suddenly didn't see the point in standing. Maybe a nap. Naps were good.

A knock sounded at the door.

She peeked, trying to open her eyes.

"Is that them, Mom?"

Maddie couldn't be sure, but she was pretty sure her mother nodded.

So tired.

"Trust me. Trust in Kal."

"Yeah. Sure, mom. Suck my energy. I'll trust you." Maddie was so damn tired though. Honestly, she didn't think she could panic right now if she wanted to.

Getting up failed once, twice, and then, nope. She rolled over onto all fours and started to crawl.

Another knock.

Impatient much? She'd get there when she damn well got there.

When had that damn door gotten so far?

Fumbling at the lock, she pulled it open with a creak.

"Hello?" she asked.

Blinking at the brightest damn sun, Maddie fought to see against the light streaming through.

"Maddie? Are you alone?"

She blinked again. His voice. So familiar.

So tired.

Maddie nodded as she slid back down the door propping her up. Her arms shook in exhaustion. Nope, she wasn't staying up. That was fine. The floor was now her friend.

"Maddie? On my God! What did that monster do to you?"

Her head rolled back and forth. Who the hell was at her door? The voice it was so familiar.

Oh, right. Light bulb moment. "Donnie?"

She tried to focus on the dark blob at the door, looking up into his face.

"Of course it's Donnie. Who else would it be?"

Her head was really heavy. Maddie fought against her will and the weakness in her muscles as her heavy head lolled to the left. Then she pulled her head to the right. Well, this wasn't going as planned. Wait, what was the plan? Was there a plan?

"Maddie. Come here. Are you drunk?"

What had he just asked? Everything was static.

"What? Drunk? No. So tired."

Muffled voices in the background had her trying to force herself to focus. Stupid witches. Think Maddie. Think. When in doubt just repeat shit you've heard, right? She giggled. Okay, maybe she was drunk.

"Donnie? Are you alone?" Her words might have had a bit of a slur. She'd curse at her mom later.

"What? No. Why would I be alone to come face to face with a monster? I'm here to save you."

Save? No.

"No. No. I don't need to be saved."

Unwelcome hands wrapped around her and started to pull her up.

"I beg to differ. The son of a bitch alien has done something to you."

The words took a few seconds to process.

"No. Well, maybe. In bed." She started to giggle again. Fuck. What had her mother done?

So tired.

"Don't drop me, okay?" was all she said as her legs buckled.

Surprisingly, he didn't. Maybe she should have given Donnie more credit.

That elicited a snort from her. Ha, ladylike.

It didn't matter. Donnie still couldn't hold a candle to Kal. "Ha. Candle."

Donnie gripped her harder and although it felt wrong, Maddie couldn't stop laughing.

"What? What candle," Donnie asked.

Maddie stopped laughing and couldn't hold her head up. No more jokes. She needed to save the energy she had.

"Someone help, already," said Donnie.

Maddie heard another person, someone she didn't know.

"What the hell is wrong with her? Is she even going to be able to help us?"

A few grunts and groans before Maddie felt someone else lifting her feet. Kal wouldn't need help. Her eyelids felt so heavy. Maybe she should just sleep. Yes, sleep. Her mother said not to use her magic, anyway. Although, right now she wasn't even sure her mother had left any magic at all.

Her feet lifted, someone grabbed her butt, and then she was sitting. That was rude. Leaning over, she sort of sat, sort of leaned. What the hell?

Oh, right. This is what it felt like to be shoved into a car. Wait. No. This was bad.

"Maddie? What is wrong with you? We can't help if we don't know."

Who was 'we'? Donnie had a we?

"Sh-murph."

"What? Smurf? What the hell was that."

Taking some borrowed energy from God knows where, she raised her arm and scratched her nose. It itched.

"What is wrong with you?"

"I had an Ishhh."

"What?"

How did Donnie not get that she had an itch? Sighing, she let her head rest against whatever sat next to her. Probably Donnie. Probably not the vibe she needed to set.

"Let's go. Whatever he did to her needs to wear off. Head to the compound and we can figure it out later. He's not going to leave without her. Let's get her safe and then set the trap."

Maddie couldn't make her lips work. She couldn't tell him to fuck off or even to just sit further away. So she listened.

"She better be able to help. You know that the doctor is expecting us to retrieve these guys. If we have to use your girlfriend as bait, so be it."

Maddie's head shifted as the shoulder she'd leaned against moved.

"She isn't bait. I told you he will come for her. You should see the way he was controlling her."

Maddie thought of Kal. Maybe he could hear her from here. She didn't really understand any of it, but she didn't want him to come for her. She didn't want him to get caught.

"Look at her. That thing did more than just a mind game on her," said a voice that wasn't Donnie.

"Those are the fucking tattoos I mentioned. Although I didn't know they glowed like this until last night. What the fuck is he? Is she infected? Can you fix her?"

Gravel kicked up outside of what she now knew was a car. The engine revved.

"Fuck. I don't know. Let's report back. They'll want to see this," said the same new voice.

Maddie sat somewhere between sleep and awake. Maybe this was all a bad dream; then again if Kal wasn't a dream this probably wasn't a nightmare.

No one else said anything until the car stopped.

Maddie let everything happen to her like she was observing, not that she had any other choice.

"I'll get her. Just don't. No one's allowed to touch her without my permission. That's the agreement and for now that's how it will be," said Donnie.

"Whatever Reyes. You better not fuck this up. You have no idea how this alien could catapult our sector within the Illuminati. You have no idea how much money is riding on this research."

Maddie wanted to ask Donnie who was talking. Reyes was his last name, but why was it used in a sentence with Illuminati. Wait, were they real? She'd heard of them, crazy conspiracy theorists that supposedly had their people in every government in the world. But they weren't real. Where was she?

Maddie tried to talk, instead she was sure it sounded like a drunken stupor. Or maybe nothing came out. Who knows? Exhaustion pulled at her eyelids. It would be so easy to give in.

Using her mind, she called out to Kal.

Don't come for me.

That should work. She hoped.

Forcing her eyes open, Maddie winced. The heat of the sun licked at her skin, bringing her some comfort.

Daylight. That had to mean they weren't too far or at least too many hours hadn't passed.

"Get her inside, Reyes. They'll want an update."

That was it. Maddie decided once she was strong again,

she'd be turning that asshole into a cockroach. He sounded like one.

Footfalls crunched against whatever covered the ground, dirt she supposed. A few seconds ticked by before she was jostled in Donnie's arms. At least it was more graceful than her initial kidnapping. He was going to get it, just as soon as she could magic up something, anything. Maddie shivered as the temperature changed to the cool of air conditioning.

"Take her down below. Put her in a cell for observation," said another voice. Maddie couldn't move her head enough to see who it was. A girl this time, maybe?

"Oh, hey. Look at that. She's coming to," said the cockroach-man from earlier.

"Where am I?"

Donnie pulled her in protectively, and she tried to wiggle away. Donnie had never been that strong, but right now she wasn't going anywhere.

"You're at our headquarters. Just stay quiet and I'll get you out of here alive," Donnie whispered.

Well, shit. That didn't sound good.

"I'm not taking her to a cell. She'll do fine in a guest room. I'll stay with her and see what I can find out. In the meantime, post some guys outside. If that alien comes, you don't know what he's capable of."

Maddie tried to call out again to Kal, trying to tell him to stay away. Everything in her was muted. What if he couldn't hear her? Maybe he wouldn't come if he couldn't track her. If only they could have waited to kidnap her for a few more days. Super inconvenient to not understand her new powers.

She giggled to herself.

Yeah, she sounded drunk. Maybe the panic would set in soon enough.

"Shit, she glows?" someone asked.

Donnie's voice spoke up. "No she doesn't fucking glow. It's something he did."

"Maybe she should go straight to the lab," said the girl.

Maddie decided that woman would be a cockroach too or maybe a praying mantis. She seemed like a huge man-eater.

"No. I'm not taking her to the lab. The agreement was that I would get him if she was protected. I said I knew how to get the alien, but she was supposed to be protected."

The woman's voice said again, "yeah, that was before we knew she was one of them."

Maddie could almost feel the anger rolling off of Donnie. "She isn't. I told you she's human. Her mother was one of those clairvoyants in town. She's just human. A telekinetic, but that's about it. She's not rare to this organization and you only need her to get that fucking alien."

Silence fell for a minute. Maddie might consider thanking Donnie later for saving her, but then again it sounded like he'd just sold her and Kal out.

"Fine. Take her down. Find out what she knows."

*K*al clutched his chest as a string of pain ripped through him.

"Kal? You okay?" Eadric asked.

It took him a second to catch his breath.

"Yeah. No." Flexing his back, he rolled his shoulders, trying to release the tension.

The chair fell to the ground with a crack as he abruptly stood. "It's Maddie. Something's happened."

Five sets of eyes, all glowing and on alert settled on him.

"Can you reach her?" asked Barak.

Kal tried to sense her. Their connection was weak, and that only meant that she was alive, but surely not okay.

He closed his eyes, pushing away everything but her. He tried to follow the threads only he could see. So weak.

"No. I can't. She's not far, but she's weak. Something's happened."

His dragon woke, spreading his wings. Kal allowed him to take some control, see if he could sense anything new.

Stretching his hands as their claws sat just below the surface. Nothing.

"I can't sense her. I felt a shot of panic and pain. I don't understand what's happened. I need to go."

Kal stepped off the ship and out into the same familiar surrounding of the desert. They'd moved the ship a few miles away, enough to throw off some sniffing lab coats. No one had found them, but it was too close for comfort.

It had been a good call to allow Cy to remain with the ship. He'd get his turn soon enough, but he was the most trained in emergency proceedings. Too bad right now that was of no comfort to Kal.

"I thought this planet knew nothing of us?" he screamed back.

Sucking in the air, fighting back the rage, the shift, he waited for a plan to come to him.

"How is it that within a matter of a day they're sniffing up our asses? Is it coincidence that some strange people were out here and now my mate is in danger?" Kal growled.

He started pacing in the sand. "I can't get a read on her."

Eadric came up beside him. "That mate of yours is strong. I'm sure she can handle herself. But, as soon as you have a read, I'll fly with you. Just keep her from turning me into some kind of bird."

Everyone laughed, except Kal. He couldn't. Her life was in danger. There was no doubt.

"I'm shifting. My dragon might have a better chance of hearing her."

They all backed away as Kal's skin burned away into scales.

The air parted as his wings tore free. Rearing up on his hind legs, he prepared for battle. His dragon landed back on all fours, sniffing the air, listening for her. His brothers all stared intently at him.

Just as he was about to say there was nothing new, a weak sound of her voice came to him.

Don't come for me. They want you.

He stopped thrashing about, waiting. Nothing. The dragon growled.

Eadric crawled up alongside him, ready to take flight in his own dragon form.

Someone has her. They want us.

Sniffing the air, he tried to make out her magic. The air too thick with other magic that he could pick out her, but that didn't seem right. This town would be a curse just as much as it was his blessing. He wouldn't be able to make her out, not clearly, not from here. Not if she was weak.

I'm going to her house. We need to start there.

Eadric's massive head nodded, the red-hued skin and wings unique just as Kal's orange was to him. They all had a unique color on their underbellies, yet all were similar in so many ways.

I will follow. Eadric said within their minds.

The other four stood and nodded.

We will wait for your call. Responded Cy.

Kal watched as Deo stood in the way.

You do not take on the enemy without reporting back first. We weren't aware of any threats.

Kal nodded his massive head and pushed up into the sky, shimmering as he camouflaged to the Earth's darkening sky.

The ground passed quickly, but to Kal the clock had stopped. The Earth stood still.

They covered the miles between their ship and her home in a matter of minutes, and his heart stopped as he caught the familiar sight. He opened his senses further, trying to feel for her. Something. Anything. Yet nothing. They circled as Kal tried to figure out what else to do.

A moment later her weak voice came through to him again. Fading in and out.

Run, Kal. Donnie is part of it. He told them about you. Run. I'll be fine.

Like fucking hell he'd leave her. Eadric nodded as Kal relayed the same information. He could sense her now. Still weak, but he felt her.

The dragon flicked its head toward the mountains. Not far at all. He would find her and then, Donnie would regret his choice.

Both dragons turned and took off into the distance. He was coming for her. He would find her. And he would kill whoever had threatened her. This was what he was bred for. This was the monster he knew.

Kal and Eadric touched down near what appeared to be a house. Nothing but a damn house. The mountain air chilled his dragon's soul, or maybe that was the loss of his mate. The two dragons tucked in between trees, trying to hide their size among green and brown foliage. Fuck, they stuck out like two dragons in a damn forest.

His dragon sniffed the air and snorted. Her scent lingered. Eadric whipped his head around, back and forth, as they tried to hide while still seeking Maddie.

There was nothing happening. Kal's dragon dug his claws into the ground, digging up a chunk of earth and letting each grain drain through his massive claws.

He needed to remain calm, come at this as a highly skilled warrior rather than a lovesick pup.

His dragon gave a chest-deep rumble in response. They both needed her and emotion would save no one.

The unassuming white and black exterior was out of place, but how? Narrowing his eyes, his dragon listened. Heartbeats. The hunter within him could feel them.

Maddie?

He tried again through the weak connection.

Nothing. They, Kal and Eadric, used their power to feel, looking for magic.

Moments passed, sitting and waiting. Studying, waiting for what they knew was there to show itself.

Floods of colors danced along the air. So many types of magic. Their dragons snorted and crouched lower, waiting for a target.

Kal snarled at the lack of Maddie's signature. His dragon scanned the area once more, and he had to do a double take as something faint faded with every passing second. There. That was her.

Tucking his wings close to his body, they prowled low and paused. There was no way to go unnoticed once they left the cover of the trees.

Kal gave Eadric a quick nod, and they shifted into human form.

Just as quick as they shifted, they both ducked and ran for the cover of a vehicle.

"What kind of place is this?" Kal said.

Eadric sniffed the air. "I don't know. Can't be anything good though. There are a lot of scents I don't recognize. Human, but not."

Kal studied the building.

There's more to this place than what we can see. I hear an elevator. Do you see any type of monitoring system?

Eadric pointed.

There and there. The words strong in Kal's head.

Nodding, Kal held out his hand. A lick of fire flared up. He blew on it and it took off towards camera one. Eadric did the same to the next. Both cameras out of commission, they stood and moved.

Don't come here, Kal. Please stay. I'm safe.

Her voice stopped him. He could feel her fear, how was she safe. This time, he was close enough that even with the weak connection her fear spilled through.

She was not safe; she was not even close to safe. He could feel what she wouldn't say, there was no hiding it.

Eadric went to take a step forward and Kal held him back.

She's telling me to stay away. What the hell am I supposed to do?

The sun was nearly gone now, time was passing. Time. Fuck, he hated time.

Call out to her again. See if she answers? Ask her why?

Nodding, Kal calmed his mind. Right.

Maddie?

The echoing of her voice came through weak.

Kal? Please go. They want you. They'll want your brothers if they find you.

Kal looked at Eadric.

Who's they?

She was quiet again for a few heart beats.

What's she saying? Eadric asked.

Kal shook his head. "Hold on. She's quiet again."

Kal? Don't come for me. Go home.

What the-?

"She's telling us to go. But she won't tell me who has her."

Eadric took a step forward. "Ask again. And next, we don't ask, we just go in."

Maddie? Who are they?

His brother started to move.

Kal followed Eadric. "Where are you going?"

Eadric looked back at him and then at the house. "We need to save your mate. I don't think I could leave if I wanted, anyway. Something - there's something here."

Kal nodded. "Yeah. Some assholes are here. Come on. She hasn't answered. I'm no longer waiting for her permission."

Eadric smiled. *There's my brother.*

They walked in silence, slowly approaching the house, taking in any shift in the air.

Fire licked along their skin, ready for the attack.

Things were too quiet. Whatever they were up against couldn't be too bad. Nothing on this planet was known to be a galactic threat, but still her fear drove him, fueling his fire within. No one threatened him or his mate.

Kal? Go. I feel you.

Maddie's voice again.

Go. They will hurt you if you come for me.

He ground his molars at her last response.

What are they, Maddie?

Eadric and Kal stood in front of the door, staring at it.

"Do we burn it down?" Eadric asked.

"No. We don't. My mate is in there." Kal reached out. "Maybe we should try the door knob?"

Eadric leaned against the side of the house.

The knob turned.

"This is really anticlimactic, isn't it?" he said as Kal gave the door a push.

Kal's dragon sat below the surface, ready. "It's odd. Perhaps they don't really understand what they are up against? I know she's afraid, but I can't tell from what."

As Kal took a step forward, he lifted a forearm against a blast of light blinding him.

Fine, they could play dirty. Kal knew within a second Maddie was here, not exactly where. She was down. Fuck.

Eadric - it's clear. Burn them.

Kal flexed his arms and called on his dragon's powers. His skin turned to scales, his dragon remaining within as they worked together. Turning his head one way and then the other, looking for the access to a basement, and he caught Eadric as he let out a battle cry, his body engulfed in dragon fire.

Go, Kal. I'll get whoever is up here causing this strange fiery light.

Eadric charged into the white of the room with Kal on his heels.

Maddie?

Her scent fresh and stronger, he followed where she'd been stopping dead at a bookshelf. She did not just disappear. He turned in a quick circle, but there was nothing. Where had they gone? There was no more house. This was it.

Anger seethed through him. He would not give up now. No, he'd come too far for her. There was something he missed.

Kal gripped the edges of the taunting bookcase and ripped it away. Surprise hit him as an odd door surfaced. Maddie was behind here, and this door was the only thing between him and his mate.

Fueled by his need to protect her, Kal pushed at it. Metal.

Claws extended from his hands and he began to rip at the cold and unforgiving material. It would not stop him. Kal stopped and scowled at the marred surface. Too slow. Something else. There had to be another way in. Some other way to force this door to open. It was then that a small green light on the right side caught his eye.

Eadric? I need something. A key card I would assume.

A moment later something smacked him in the back of the head.

Here. Now hurry up.

Kal swiped up the card from the floor. It was only then that Kal noticed the blaze around them out in the main room. So much for quiet.

Shoving the key card against the smaller rectangle, his patience wore thin. Finally the pad and the doors parted. Of course. How stupid could he be when his mate was involved. Stupid. He couldn't do that. A second passed as he cleared his mind.

An elevator the size of a fucking shower greeted him. His dragon growled. Yeah. No. They wouldn't be shifting; not in here.

Getting in, he turned and saw several buttons. Great. Which floor. Stepping back, Kal relaxed his mind. Blowing out a breath, anything to calm his heart, the blood pumping through his veins, and the anger surging through him. She was here, he just had to sense her. The door closed and for a moment he stood there. The quieter he was, the louder she came through as he searched floor by floor. Room, by room, her heartbeat finally echoing back like a beacon. Pressing the button, he prepared for an attack as he descended.

His dragon crouched within him, ready. Their skin thick with dragon scales still, his eyes-battle ready to hunt by body heat rather than by human sight. Kal sat in balance between human-warrior and dragon-warrior.

Pushing up against the wall with nowhere else to hide, he did what he could.

The doors opened, and before he took his next breath something growled, lunging in to attack. Kal snapped out a hand, and the figure began to scream as he incinerated it within seconds. Another figure came out of a fog and Kal simply reached out again. This time a knife sparked against his armor as the person ignited and screamed.

Maddie's voice broke the screaming and sounds of confusion beyond the tin can fortress.

Kal? They have magic. I can't protect you.

He squeezed his fists against the change, his claws trying to break through. He didn't give a damn what they had. They would not stand in the way between him and Maddie.

I've seen the magic. It hasn't helped them. I'm coming. He said back.

Reaching for her through their connection, he allowed her emotions to flow through him. Her anger, her fear, and underneath it all, hope. He'd never let her out of his sight again.

From the corner of his eye, more movement.

"Stay right there," said a voice.

Standing still, he turned his head and glared. Who the hell had the right to tell him to stay, like some pet.

"Tell me where Maddie is and perhaps I will do as you ask."

Three men walked out of the fog like the mist taking on form, guns pointing in his direction.

"She's safe, for now. As long as you cooperate, maybe you'll see her again."

His dragon didn't like those words one bit. Neither did Kal nor the roar that he screamed into the space.

Stretching to his full height, he unfolded from the elevator. The mist clouded the room and he couldn't make out the full size of what he believed to be a hall. Morphing into something between the dragon and the human, the stench of fear permeated his nostrils. Kal let more of his dragon come out to play, but only enough that they could still move.

"W-what the fuck is that?"

Much better, he thought to himself.

The humans started to shoot at him, the bullets more dart-like. They bounced off his scales. Very little on this planet could hurt him, and he had every intention of showing them exactly how useless their weapons were.

Kal sucked down the air, slowly tasting it, feasting on the smell of terror. It was a drug to his beast. They lived for this shit.

Fire brewed within him with every step he took. He'd taunt them. A second later and Kal began to torch the room, filling any space between him and the men with fire. Heat signatures of human and not-so-human scattered. The mist might have blinded him as a man, but not as a dragon.

The attack stopped, and he sprang into action. Kal used his dragon sense to sniff out threats. He needed to understand his enemies, but more, he was trying to figure out where Maddie was imprisoned. So close, yes, Maddie was weak. What had they done to her?

Kal would know her presence for the rest of his life, and the thought she was so close and yet so far pissed him off even more. She would be back in his arms soon.

Standing without cover wasn't ideal. Scanning around the space, the colder spots told him where walls and voids were beyond the airy fog. Nowhere much to hide. Alright then.

He started to walk. To Kal's surprise the fog began to

clear, revealing a hall that appeared to be much larger than the small house above. Stark white doors, the only decoration on either side with small letters and numbers. Nothing helpful.

The dragon drank in the terror that continued to fill the air, thick and heavy. At least someone was smart.

The hall seemed empty though, so somewhere, perhaps behind these doors, were more humans or something like a human. Come out, come out and play, he thought.

Kal stalked through the remaining smoke cover, following the strongest sense of her.

"I wouldn't go any further, alien," an overhead speaker blared.

Turning his head back and forth, Kal tried to locate the source. Small little domes covered what must have been cameras, and near them were speakers he'd missed in all the excitement. One on either end of the long space.

He pulled back his dragon to allow himself the ability to speak. "Oh? And why is that?"

"We don't need any trouble. We're merely interested in your species."

Really? Doubtful.

When he didn't speak, the voice spoke up again.

"Let me introduce myself. I'm Dr. Rollings. This is a research facility. We have no intention of hurting you, as long as you stop this little attack."

This time Kal snorted. "Attack? You attacked me. You took my mate. Hand her over and we leave."

The crackle of the speaker sounded on and off and on again. "Mate? We were under the impression she was human."

Officially annoyed, Kal rolled his eyes. He didn't have time for this, and he continued his search, stopping at each door.

The first door didn't have her scent. The second was more of the same. And the third.

"You won't find her, this facility is state of the art. The Illuminati are nothing if not thorough in their endeavors."

He stopped. Kal scraped his claws against the door. It dented, just as anything would under his attack.

"Illumi-what? I don't care what you are. You do not threaten me, my mate, or my kind."

A door opened behind him.

"Stop, alien."

He didn't bother turning around. The fire did as he asked and took the enemy behind him so he could continue on his search for his mate.

*M*addie woke with a start. When had she fallen asleep? Tired. She was still so tired. She tried to push herself up but her limbs acted more like lead weights than appendages. Stupid body. Flopping her head back down again, she squeezed her eyes shut against the exhaustion.

Okay. What had all happened. This was stupid. A spell. She needed something that would give her a caffeine jolt in magic form.

Whispering a few words, she waited. Well, if she didn't exactly have magic to cast more magic, maybe her fate would be to just lay there. All right. Back to the basics. She remembered coming somewhere.

She remembered telling Kal to stay. Yeah. That was probably a fruitless effort. Oh, right. Every time she spent energy to contact him she'd pretty much pass out.

What else had happened? Maddie had a long list of people being turned into cockroaches. She also had a cocktail of feelings toward her ex, none of which didn't also have him ending up like a cockroach. So, now. Kal? Where was he? He'd gone to his brothers. Right. And then her mother visited.

Right, her mom. Reality came back. Her mom had done something. Sucked her dry of all energy. And then, what was next? Right, Donnie had kidnapped her. Great. She was all caught up and now she could be pissed.

Blinking, Maddie tried to make out shapes. The lights a blinding white didn't help her throbbing head. Where had that little douche-canoe taken her? At least she was alone right now. Her skin crawled thinking of being in his arms. How had she ever thought of marrying him? When had that ever been a good idea?

There are moments when something solidifies your choices. This was that moment where all guilt could leave. Her anger ate up all the space she'd saved for remorse. He'd never have made her happy, and she sure as hell would never have let him control her.

Fear of being lonely was nasty. Her life had felt like she was always running into a dark room with no idea where to go or what was in front of her. She was always looking for something, or someone. Reality was that she would never find what she needed, not by running. Her show had been a failure, but probably because she'd been looking for answers that weren't there.

Everyone wanted answers to the afterlife, but maybe any answer would never be enough. Because the dead couldn't answer why them and not you.

It was finding your purpose. Finding your why. The reason you were alive, left behind. She'd lived for so long in a fog, and then Kal came in and suddenly everything became bright. She could see everything.

Good. Finally. So, instead of feeling sad for herself, she

needed to get her shit together and get out of wherever Donnie had brought her.

She would focus on moving one finger at a time.

Well, hell. Panting with exhaustion, the shitty reality crept in. This could take a while.

The door creaked, freezing her blood. Or well, she stopped moving her fingers.

The door clicked shut a second later. Listening, Maddie could hear footsteps.

"Maddie? Are you awake?"

Her stomach pitched. Donnie's voice was the last one she'd ever wanted to hear again.

Okay. So. Did she answer or not? Would he just go away?

"Maddie? I can see your heart rate on the monitor. I know you're awake."

Well, crap.

"Fine. I'm awake. Why are you spying on my heart, anyway?"

Maddie had never realized how unnervingly quiet he moved. The shift of the mattress shook her, and if she could have jumped up and away, she'd have done it.

"You're acting weird. I had to do something. A nurse came in and hooked you up to a monitor. Nothing else though. If we don't know what he did, we can't treat it. I didn't let them draw blood, not yet."

Her eyes flew open at the blinding light. Blinking a few times, she finally focused and saw Donnie was way too close for comfort.

"Yeah. You better not have let them draw my blood. They are crazy. Right? All of them; are nuts? Talking about aliens."

The bed shifted as Donnie moved closer. Maddie attempted to back away, managing a few inches.

"Maddie, don't be like that. They are here to keep us all safe. Well, I should say we. I signed on to help them."

Of course he did.

"Right. You always did make dumb choices." Maddie moved her arm. The fact he was so close gave her the drive to move the stupid appendage.

Maddie? Which room are you in?

Her breath hitched, and Maddie tried to cough to hide it. Kal. Of course he was here. It would be a lie to say she wasn't relieved.

"Maddie. What has gotten into you? I get it. You're mad, but it's only because you're not yourself. That alien did something to you."

She tried to laugh, but it hurt. She couldn't let Kal walk in with Donnie here. That was all she needed, some kind of male pissing contest. Donnie would lose, but she didn't need that on her.

"Fine, Donnie. Fine. Do you want me to admit he's not from here? Fine. He's not. But stop assuming he did anything. He has not hurt me."

Deep breaths. One, two. And up she went.

"See. I'm sitting up, just like a big girl." Well, shit. Now she wanted another nap.

I don't know where I am. Donnie's here. Maybe search for the scent of deceit?

She could practically feel the laugher in Kal. Hell, maybe she really could.

Through the exhaustion there was something new, maybe some kind of energy. Was her magic recovering? Bits of energy, like a leak in a dam trickled through her. Thank God. Kal. It had to be Kal's energy finding its way to her.

"Maddie? Are you listening?"

Ugh. Could she just say no?

"Sorry. What?"

His hand rested on her leg. Her eyes narrowed.

"I asked you, if you remembered what happened. What he - I mean, when did you start feeling this way?"

She bit her lip, trying to stop from swearing at him. At least until Kal got there.

"Can you move your hand, please?"

He smirked.

"Do you even realize the only reason you're not a guinea pig is because they believe you to be my fiancé still?"

She sat there thinking of how it would look when Kal punched him.

"Which, I know you'd change your mind if he weren't here brainwashing you. So, before you yell. Yes. I know. You haven't agreed to anything yet."

Wow. He just didn't get it. All the missed calls that she never returned. The returned Christmas gift. The holiday card she'd sent with a picture of her and her TV crew with no mention of coming home. Nothing. And yet, nothing had told him she'd meant it when she'd said they were wrong for each other.

"Donnie. Stop. Please. Stop lying to yourself. I appreciate your attempt to save my life from something you delivered me to. Which, we will need to talk about in a second. It's sort of backhanded to say that I'm safe because of you. I'm also in deep shit because of you. I think that sort of outweighs it all."

His hand slid a little higher. She twitched her leg, and he didn't move. Donnie's face twisted into something much more fae than human. More sinister than she'd ever seen.

"You don't seem to understand. He, your alien, put you in this position. He put me in this position. That alien took you from me and gave me no choice. I would have left him alone, I wouldn't have joined this stupid group. But, I didn't have a choice now, did I?"

Maddie dug her nails into the bed, trying to pull herself away.

Donnie twisted from where he sat and began to climb up the bed. One hand on either side of her. She lay back, avoiding his face. He hovered over her, her heart rate kicking up in panic.

"What does he have that I don't? Is this what you want? A man to take what he wants? Some alpha a-hole prick? I'd be more than happy to play this little game."

Fear gripped her. A spell, something. She tried to cast a transformation spell. Nothing. She tried to conjure up the fire that Kal had taught her to manipulate, but all she could feel was a sputtering of sparks on her fingers. Crap.

"Donnie. No. That's not what he's about."

He pushed a knee between her legs.

She couldn't breathe.

"Donnie. I can't fight you off. This is rape. I'm not willing."

He smirked.

"Is that the way you like it? I saw you run from him in the alley. And yet, you were still back with him? He's an asshole. Maybe all those experts are right. The nice guy finishes last. Not this time, Madeline. Not this time."

Donnie lowered his head, his eyes flashing a creepy inhuman gold.

Maddie turned her head, his words a sickening heat against her ear.

"Do you think he will still want you with another man's scent on you? Do you think he'll still want you with another's magic flowing within you?"

She squirmed. "Ew, gross. Get off, Donnie."

Pushing him, he didn't move. She was no match, not in her still-drained body.

"You didn't think I was gross a few years ago."

The sour in the pit of her stomach came back, the same as it had every time she'd been with him or any man for that fact. She had known deep down they weren't right for her, her own version of her mother's power, maybe.

Okay. This wasn't working. Maybe she could change tactics. Fae magic wasn't in her expertise, and she couldn't use it to power her own. The sting of something foreign pricked her skin. It had to be Donnie.

She had to breathe, but the feeling brought up panic. Dread. This wasn't right.

She winced as Kal's anger raced through her, at the realization that she couldn't hide anything from him. Anger wasn't solving this though, and she needed to change her tactics with Donnie.

"Donnie. Stop. I. I mean. What kind of relationship could we have if we start off like this?"

He paused.

Good. That had to be good.

"Just think about it. I mean, you obviously believe I can't live without you. But, how can you prove that if I'm angry? If he has me under a spell, I won't be able to think rationally, not when it comes to you or any other man," she said.

Donnie pushed himself up, giving her space to look at him.

"Right?" Maddie asked.

She didn't like the way his eyes flicked over her.

"I can't figure out what he's done. What if it's a spell. What if ..." He died off.

"What if wha-"

He pressed his lips against hers and Maddie freaked out. She couldn't push him away. She couldn't get him off of her, but as she pressed her fingers against his skin, she called out to Kal's powers.

A tear slid, running down her temple as she focused on the threads of fire coming to her. She could feel the warmth growing, growing.

Finally, Donnie jumped back with a scream. "You bitch."

She bit back the tears. "Don't you ever touch me again."

Donnie wasn't Donnie anymore. His skin tinged an inhuman green.

"If I can't have you, no one can."

Maddie held on to whatever energy she could, pushing herself further up on the bed, calling the fire to her. She focused on the holes in his shirt where her fingers had singed the fabric.

"Donnie, you never had me."

He snarled. Maddie had never seen what a half-breed might look like, but she supposed this was the Fae nature. Jealous. Fickle.

He took a step towards her. Her skin began to burn, the fire was coming to protect her. She would do whatever it took to get back to her dragon, her Kal, her mate.

A thunderous roar filled the room as the door dented.

He was here.

a battle cry ripped from him as he rammed into the door.

Fuck. All he'd done was dent the fucking thing. This wasn't working.

Think. He needed to be smarter than these humans. Scanning the door, another small pad caught his eye. He slammed the keycard on it. A red light lit up. Of course it did. Stupid humans.

Nothing would stand between him and his mate. Anger shook him as Maddie's emotions ripped through him like torrential rains. Her desperation. Disgust. Fear.

Think. What did he have? He wasn't the brains of the group; he was the brawn. And right now, the brawn was losing the damn fight. He ripped at the panel with his claws.

Colored wires.Wonderful.

Cy, what wire controls the circuit.

Within a second he got his answer.

Try purple. Most of the tech here is magnet based.

Kal growled.

I don't care what it is.

He searched the panel. Red, Green. Something that might be purple.

You care, Kal. You need to cut the power.

He followed the wire. It looked different. Sure. Why not? Leaning in, he sniffed the cable. It had an electrical scent stronger than any other. Hesitation took a leap off a cliff as a rip of pain hit him in the heart. Fuck it.

He sliced through the purple wire.

A buzzing sound stopped and then he heard a click.

One more time, he was getting to her if he had to rip the entire building apart. Kal shoved his shoulder into the door once more, this time the door swung open.

Maddie lay on a bed, the surrounding fabric singed.

The asshole in front of him however, did not look okay. No. In Kal's head he was already dead.

"You touched my mate," he growled.

Donnie seemed to uncurl and grow an inch or two, but Kal really didn't see the difference as he looked down on the small halfling creature. He didn't care what Donnie was or how big he tried to be.

"She isn't yours. You can't just claim her like property."

Donnie paused, a sneer spreading across his lips.

"I already tried, and she doesn't seem to tolerate that."

Kal's eyes grew wide.

He glanced from Maddie to Donnie.

She started to whimpier. "Kal. Just take me out of here. Ignore him. Just get us out of here."

His heart broke. The scent of her terror curled his nose. Why wasn't she coming to him? Reaching for her in his mind, the emotions rushed in clearly. Exhaustion. Weakness. Terror. Relief. It just kept coming.

"What have you done to her?" he growled.

Donnie postured. Kal knew what battle looked like. He knew what someone asking for a fight looked like, and Donnie was asking for it. Kal took a step closer and retracted his claws. He would beat this whiny human man-to-man.

Donnie backed up. "Don't come near me, asshole. This place is one giant trap for you. There is nowhere for you to go."

"I don't think you understand what a trap is. It won't matter when I rip your head off. Did you touch my mate?"

Out of the corner of his eye, Maddie moved. Slowly.

Good goddess, he'd make Donnie pay.

"She isn't yours, alien. And, if you must know. Yes. I kissed her."

A rage boiled within him. Before Donnie could blink, Kal clenched Donnie's throat between his fingers. Kal lifted him off the ground, his feet dangling.

There was no controlling his dragon now. Razor-sharp teeth filled his mouth and the urge to rip this creature to shreds took over any human logic.

"Kal, stop!" screamed Maddie.

Her voice broke through the blinding rage. He turned. Maddie wasn't on the bed anymore. How had he missed this? How had he missed the attack on his mate?

"Drop him," said another voice.

Kal did as commanded and Donnie hit the ground with a thunk.

"Very good. Very good. He's like a trained dog," said a guard.

There was only one in the room, but he had Maddie.

The dragon retreated, enough that Kal was more human than beast.

The guard backed into the hallway with Kal following. He would not lose his mate. "Release her," he commanded.

Stepping into the hall revealed more and more humans.

Of course. He should have known.

Eadric. Where are you?

Out in the hall, the guard retreated into the small throng of white lab coats.

"Now, now. There is no reason for violence."

Kal really wanted to go rip some throats out, and he damn near did, stopping at the sight of the gun pressed against Maddie's head.

Her eyes, large saucers, her body rigid. This wasn't his Maddie.

I will save you.

She tried to force a smile.

Yeah. Could you do it a little faster then?

He chuckled.

"What's so funny?" said a ragged voice beside him.

Donnie climbed out of the room, his hand around his neck.

He would die, if it was the last thing Kal ever did. Donnie would die.

Kal. Ignore him. Just get us out of here.

Ignore him? How? Fuck. Having a mate did complicate things. Kal tried to center himself, his soul. They needed to think straight. His dragon needed to be the brains right now. Take the emotion out of it. He couldn't though. He needed her. A new feeling spiraled through him. Desperation.

Why the fuck did the goddess give them all the power of the universe and yet require this? A mate. A balance. She was his weakness. He had something to lose, something other than himself.

Fuck. This was a big day. Not only did the world not revolve around him, he didn't care about his own safety anymore.

Kal backed down long enough for Donnie to get with the others.

What should they do? Maddie would be protected against his fire-

No.

Kal curled up his nose.

What do you mean, no?

Maddie's voice came to him again.

Do not just torch the place. Not without reason.

Well, that just pissed him off.

You're in danger. That's a damn good reason.

He watched her face. Her eyes glazed over. Shit. She was going to fall.

And she did. Right into Donnie's arms.

A jealousy like none other flew through him. He was supposed to be the one catching her. Anyone else at this point would have been better than that thing.

"Remove your hands from my mate."

Donnie snarled back. "Stop calling her that." His voice still weakened. At least Kal had done some damage. Not nearly enough though. The fool was still walking.

Okay. Head on straight. Head on straight.

Where the hell was Eadric?

Whatever.

Okay. What would Maddie do? These were humans. They did things like talk it out or something dumb.

"I apologize for destroying some shit. Can I please have my mate back?"

There. That was good, right?

139

Kal? What are you doing? Maddie thought.

He smiled at her and nodded. He was doing what humans did. Or, that's what he thought.

"You keep using this term. Mate. I'd like to understand what you mean by this? We see you have a somewhat reptilian look to you. She is obviously human in some capacity."

Donnie barked at the guy. "She is human."

The older man nodded. "Yes. Yes. So you have led us to believe."

Kal's patience was wearing.

"Enough. Release her. Now." He stopped and then thought better. "Please."

The older man smiled. "No. I'm afraid right now that won't work. You see, right now you are not attacking my men. I don't believe that we are safe if we release this woman."

He balled his hands and stood straight. He needed to control his next answer. The gun had disappeared from the back of her head. The negative, she was in Donnie's grip. The positive was he saw a way out.

Eadric? Whatever you do, don't come down here.

His plan was in motion. Only, maybe it was Maddie's plan he was hearing.

14

*M*addie elbowed Donnie. He recoiled back. Maddie would cry about all this later. She could see it plainly on Kal's face. He wasn't thinking clearly. Not thinking like someone who was a highly trained warrior, and she knew it was because of her. Maddie was his kryptonite. Damn it if she was going to be the cause of her own superman's death.

Donnie didn't fight back this time. She braced herself on the wall, trying to fake a strength she didn't have. A moment to think as everyone stared each other down.

They were getting out of here. Right after her head stopped thinking the world was a top. Damn it to hell.

How was she such a damn nightmare right now? This all still seemed to be happening to her, rather than being a participant. It was all a bad shitty nightmare that needed to end.

Kal had come for her, he'd done his part. Now she needed to get him out of here.

Focus. A quick shake of the head and she could at least see

clear. This was the hangover stage of a magic drain. Great. Her mother was going to die all over again; if Maddie got out of this, anyway.

Slapping her palm to the wall, she closed her eyes, keeping everything from turning and twisting.

The pain her mom had left, the hole in her heart had been the driving force for everything in her life. But now? She no longer cared about the why. Her mother had a reason and if it was to help her see that a world without Kal was no world at all, then she won. Maddie would do anything to protect him. He might not see it, but she did. Behind that tank of a man, behind the anger, was fear. He was afraid, and she hated it.

Kal watched them with a fire burning in his eyes. Maddie wanted to zap everyone and turn them all into something useful. Something without teeth. She tried to pull at the magic again. Now would be a great time to start her cockroach vendetta. Still nothing.

Useless. And now, with this last attempt, the exhaustion was hitting her again. Fighting off Donnie had been too much. No. No. She needed to do this. She needed to protect him. Her mate.

"Maddie, I'll fix this. He can't have you. All the doctor wants is that thing. They recruit witches to help this facility."

God. It was Donnie again. He needed to stop. She curled her lip. How was he not getting it?

Kal, you should start towards the exit.

She watched his face contort.

Over my dead body will I leave.

That was fair and expected. Well, best make the most of it then.

Let's hope it doesn't come to that. She tried to smile at him.

A strength that she knew could only come from Kal, started to pulse through her. Standing taller, she took in a deep breath.

"What is she doing?" asked one of the guards.

Donnie turned. "It's that thing. He's doing this to her."

Maddie scanned her arms, she was glowing again. Thank goodness, Kal would take her away soon. Somewhere where this might not be weird.

Feeling marginally better, she finally assessed her side of the hall.

Backing away, Maddie didn't like the change in the doctor's interest.

"So, you aren't powerless after all, then," said the older man. "Perhaps we need to keep you under isolation. Donnie, find out where they come from while we eliminate this other threat. We don't need him if we have her."

Donnie bristled, and as much as Maddie disliked him, backtrack, she had disliked him, and now she just hated him. But still, if he could keep her from becoming some bad science experiment maybe he wasn't useless just yet.

"Dr Rollings, she's a witch. I told you she was a witch. She just isn't powerful. I don't know what those tattoos are. They happened when he got her, but I doubt it means anything."

The wonderful, and she used that term lightly, Dr Rollings was a giant douche-canoe.

"I don't think she's being honest with you, Donnie. I also don't think she's your intended as you have led us to believe: it doesn't appear to me that she's brainwashed."

"She isn't herself. I promise you this isn't her," Donnie almost whined.

"Guards, take the female. Kill the male." Dr. Rollings began to turn his back.

A female in a white coat jumped forward. "No. Wait. We can observe mating habits as well as their powers and technology. Can you imagine? What if we can cross breed them into our own? Imagine the powers. Maybe they'd be the human weapons we've been failing to create. This is the species that our ancient texts talk about. It has to be. They're still around. Can you fathom how powerful he really is?" She shut up as Dr. Rollings shot daggers her way.

The doctor stepped closer to Maddie. She tried to slink away. Something was wrong with him. Magic began to flow through her veins like a flash flood. It was all coming back. She didn't attack though, not yet. Not until she was sure that she would stay on her feet.

Maddie's head still swam from the power drain. Dr Rollings stood a few inches from her, his breath smelled of onions and she turned her face away, but not before catching Dr. Rollings' eyes blink, only without blinking. Like an inner eyelid.

"What are you?" Maddie gasped.

He came closer. "I am someone who never quite gets the recognition that I deserve because I'm not altogether human, like you appear to be as well, if you are human at all."

His voice rose from a whisper as he put on what sounded like a practiced speech. "I had the money, but the Illuminati still stuck me here in charge of some looney operation that believes in aliens. The only positive is that I have had some success in cross breeding. You met one of my daughters upstairs."

Maddie stood a little taller as Kal's energy filled her. Almost ready. She was almost ready.

"I smell the magic on you now, my dear. I don't know how

you hid it before. I'll need to get a ward placed on you, and quickly I'm guessing."

She ground her teeth.

Calm yourself, Maddie. We will leave shortly. We need to neutralize this place.

"My, my. Perhaps you are right, Irene. Well, right about this being the species that some of our texts obsess over," cooed Dr. Rollings, his tone, almost more scary than before.

"Well, doctor. I hate to burst your bubble, but we will be leaving. I don't think you'll be getting any free shows from either of us," she said.

"I do think you are right about one of you." Dr. Rollings' fingers snapped. "Kill that one. We'll go after the male from upstairs. Perhaps we can see if she's compatible with that one or if they only mate with one. I don't really care. We just need one to see if human DNA and their alien DNA will do what we need."

They'd just said the wrong thing.

A pulse rose within her, only this wasn't hers. Kal's dragon was talking over. All caution was gone. He was ready for the fight.

"No one but me can and will ever touch her," roared Kal.

Maddie's eyes followed as the girl, Irene, backed away.

"Father? I mean Dr. Rollings. Perhaps we should call Lillyanna. Or, uh. One of the others up from the cells?"

He turned away from Maddie. "Why? He won't hurt her, and looking at her, she is indeed somewhat human. You." He pointed to one of the guards. "Run up and ensure this is being recorded. Did you see how these markings burned brighter when we mentioned the idea of breeding her with someone else?"

Maddie's blood boiled.

"You don't talk about me as if I am not here." Her hands burned, the feeling new and powerful. "You don't talk about me, like I would even think about leaving him behind. Like you can just throw me with someone and assume I'd want anything to do with them. I. Am. Not. An. Animal."

She welcomed the fire running along her arms.

Donnie stepped away. "Maddie. Stop. They swore they wouldn't hurt you. I -" He stared at her.

"Dr. Rollings. You did this. She was fine, until you started to threaten her," Donnie screamed.

Too late, Donnie. Just too late.

"Dr. Rollings? Is that your name? If you let me go now, and Kal, then I won't hurt you."

He laughed. "Do you think I am without any protection?"

She looked around him and sure enough the air seemed to shimmer around the edges. Maddie noticed though that none of the guards had this same distinction.

"Perhaps you do. But they don't."

He shrugged. "There will always be more to recruit. I may never find you again though."

The doctor nodded his head and Maddie yelped at a pinch in her arm. She looked down at a small dart.

Wonderful.

And now she was done being nice. Squeezing her hands tight, Maddie felt within herself. Transformation spells wouldn't fix this, although it could make the guards less of an issue. As the surrounding air grew warmer and warmer, her anger grew with it.

"Fine. Have it your way."

Maddie mumbled the only spell she could think of that would help protect some of them. She wasn't a murderer.

Kal, get us out of here in three, two ...one.

As if they were one, Kal half-shifted, breathing fire into the space, forcing everyone to scramble. She enchanted the only exit the doctor could get to, a wall of fire blocking them in as Kal grabbed her hand.

"Run!" she said.

The voice of the doctor echoed against the roar of flames. "You'll need me soon enough."

She didn't care to think what he meant as Kal shifted back to human and held the door at the opposite end of the fire.

She sprinted through, taking the flights of stairs as quickly as her borrowed energy would allow.

They reached the top and pushed through the door.

Tufts of smoke billowed out as they stepped into the charred remnants of a room. She winced only to realize it didn't burn or sting her eyes.

"Keep walking. You'll be fine. My magic won't let the fire harm you," said Kal.

They trudged through remains of a charred building.

"Is this you? Or was this someone else? The other one the doctor was screaming about?"

She felt the palm of Kal's hand against her lower back. Guiding her through the destruction.

"Eadric and most likely the female we encountered."

The roof, already collapsed in a few feet ahead, allowed the billows of smoke out and moonlight to sprinkle in.

"How long have I been here?"

He grunted. "Long enough. This way."

Leading her through what was once a wall she supposed, her feet crunched against gravel. Maddie remembered none of this.

"Move aside while I shift. I'll fly us back."

147

She blinked and his dragon appeared. Would she ever get used to this? He was magnificent.

Glancing around, she stepped towards him. "Wait. What about Eadric?"

He rolled his eyes and nodded his monstrous head.

He's already headed back.

She nodded and put her foot on the forepaw offered, swinging her legs over his neck.

Home.

The hard, silky scales under her hands felt like home. Although the power still beat through her, she still hadn't recovered. For the first time since she'd been taken, she allowed herself to let go. As the hard muscles of the dragon moved under her, she stopped fighting the exhaustion.

Part of her wanted to turn back, watch as the flames grow higher. She didn't though, better to focus on her new future. Rubbing the sore spot on her arm, she tried to envision where they were headed.

Don't worry about everything now.

Of course he heard her thoughts.

"I'll worry if I want to."

The dragon turned his head, one eye focused on her.

You mind your own business, she thought back.

Maddie felt his snort of defiance as his body moved under her legs.

You are my business, Mate.

The calm of him near her settled around the sting of panic from earlier. Would she ever be able to go back to Roswell, knowing these people lurked mere miles from the town? Would Roswell be safe for anyone anymore? She'd talk to the sheriff and some other witches in town when she got back, just long enough to grab the few belongings sitting in her car and leave again.

Then again, maybe it was just time to go. Perhaps he had been all they'd wanted.

She'd allow Kal to take her wherever. Mars, the moon, a new galaxy, wherever. She just needed him.

As the wind tossed her hair, she calmed and leaned in close to him.

Dreams of a place she'd never seen filtered into her head, although she swore she wasn't sleeping. A red sky overhead. Clouds blue instead of white.

She smiled as she fell asleep, her body still not quite caught up to the day's events.

Her last thought. She enjoyed playing with fire.

15

*K*al's paws sunk into the sand as he landed beside the ship.

We're back.

He shifted and Maddie nearly slid down his flank. Something was still wrong with her. He stopped as she adjusted herself, and he noticed the movement.

His brothers slowly walked out of the ship one by one.

"Is this her?" asked Deo.

Kal huffed in response. Stretching out his long neck to reach back. He nudged her with his snout. Maddie stirred as if she'd been asleep already. He watched her sit up straight and blink at him.

I'm going to shift back, can you stand?

Maddie looked around.

These are my brothers. They won't hurt you.

He smelled the air, pulling in the scent of her as she climbed down. Something smelled wrong, but neither he nor his dragon could figure out what or why. She wasn't afraid, though. At least there was that.

She staggered, and he shot out a paw. Her weakness pulsed through him. Damn, he hated to see her this way. Hopefully, now that she was with him, she'd fully recover. Maybe he could finally understand what had happened.

His dragon watched her. They both studied Maddie as she grappled with her own balance. Once Kal was certain she wasn't going to fall, he shifted. Seconds passed before he could touch her again.

The moment human hands replaced his claws, he wrapped her in his arms and pulled her against him. Only then did he look back at his brothers.

"Yes. This is Maddie. Maddie this is, well, everyone."

Leaning into him, she steadied. Her pulse thrummed through him, stronger at least than he'd felt at the strange compound they'd just destroyed.

"Wow. You're all. Well, you're all huge, aren't you?"

Kal took them in and shrugged. "How else would we protect our planets?"

"Planets? There's more than one?"

One of the other guys nodded. "We protect our solar system."

Casting a glance over her shoulder, she captured Kal's gaze. He'd allow himself to be captured by this creature anytime. How had he lived this long without her?

"I don't get any of this. But, well. I've seen weirder," she said to him, perhaps to everyone.

Kal pulled her in tighter. You will see soon enough.

Absently, he ran a hand down her side. How long had it been since he'd kissed her? Too long. Perhaps they could debrief the group later.

"I need to get her inside. She's been through a lot." It was then he realized Eadric was missing. Where had he gone now? "Where is Eadric?"

His brothers exchanged looks.

"Get off of me!"

Kal looked in the direction of the new voice.

Raising an eyebrow, he looked at Cy.

"Another one. She's on the other side of the ship."

Another one? He thought.

"Another witch. This one doesn't seem to change anyone into anything. Eadric would probably be a bug under her shoe by now if she was."

Kal expected Maddie to laugh at this, but instead he realized she was nearly asleep in his embrace, her weight against him.

"Why is she here?"

Cy hung his head. "You and Eadric sure know how to pick mates. That. Is his mate."

Kal bristled. "My mate is not the issue."

"Sure. Not now. But, when you met her she wasn't exactly what we'd call willing. Let's hope the rest of us have better luck than you two."

He pursed his lips as they glared. "Alright. Fine. The bird thing was unfortunate. But, look how fast she came around."

They all nodded. Jackasses would know soon enough, it didn't matter what hell they put you through.

A swell of sand rose up. He closed his eyes and protected Maddie. "What's going on? Sand storm? Was this on the radar?"

He heard a cough and Eadric's yell.

"Stop with the damn sand already, witch."

She growled at Eadric as the sand died abruptly.

"My name is Lillyanna. Let me go and I'll stop."

Maddie stirred.

"What's going on?"

Kal kissed the top of her head.

"It appears that Eadric absconded with the witch from the compound."

Maddie pulled free of his arms and looked around.

"Won't they come looking for her?" Maddie asked.

They all looked in Eadric's direction.

"Most likely. Nothing seems to go as planned around here. Perhaps we should continue with the mission and get out of here as quickly as possible," said Cy.

"Out of here? Like Roswell? Or…" Maddie pointed up.

Cy nodded.

"Come, mate. You need not worry. You are safe here. Let's get you to bed."

Her cheeks flushed pink.

Good. Perhaps she was coming around. Resting his hand on the small of her back, he helped her move.

"You know you're naked, right?" she asked.

A smile spread across his lips. "Very aware. Do you see a problem?"

Her steps faltered. Kal grabbed her up, lifting her in his arms.

"No." Maddie yawned. "But, don't your brothers get jealous?"

"Of what? We've trained together since we were children. Being in human form usually meant we were naked after shifting."

She smiled and leaned her head into his chest.

"Never mind. It's no fun to tease you. You really don't get human humor."

Kal growled. "I get humor just fine. What I don't get is what you are implying?"

Her finger absently made little circles on his chest.

"Tell me that you aren't all built like gods, you know, down there."

He glared down, but all he saw was Maddie. What the hell was she talking about? Taking a few more steps, he stopped.

"Mate, am I not enough for you in bed?"

She jumped and glared at him.

"What? No. For crap's sake. I just meant don't you guys have jealousy or contests to see who's bigger, or who's slept with more women. I mean, seriously. I don't want any of their mates to see you naked, that's all."

His shoulders relaxed. Kal hadn't realized her question had him tensed and ready to murder one of his brothers.

"Shush, dragon boy. You're plenty for me. I'm not sure anyone could ever come close. You've set a high standard."

Her hand rested over his heart.

"This is just going to take getting used to," she finished. Before Kal could get onto the ship, he paused at the yelling. Eadric might have one hell of a time with that one.

"Won't one of you help me? This is kidnapping. Let me go, and I won't tell anyone about you."

Deo stepped up. "Eadric, tame this one."

She gawked. "What is wrong with you? Maybe you are all just monsters like my father believes."

The girl stopped yelling long enough to rest her eyes on Kal and Maddie.

In her moment of distraction, Eadric finally caught up to her and grabbed her wrist.

"I'm not kidnapping you. If you'd just listen, you'd understand. Don't you feel anything?"

Maddie raised her head and whispered to Kal. "I've never seen her before. She seems, uh, nice?"

Kal bent his head to her ear. "Yeah. She seems like someone you'd like."

Maddie tried to sit up in his arms. "What's that supposed to mean?"

He pulled her closer and lowered his voice. "It means we have another woman that might give us more than we bargained for."

"I am the only woman you will need to worry about. He can deal with her."

Kal breathed in his mate. "You have no reason to be jealous."

She scoffed. "Ha. Jealous. Never."

She nestled into him. Safe. Finally. Now he could spend the rest of his life reassuring his mate that she was all he would ever want. All he would ever need. He paused as the girl, Lillyanna, shook free of Eadric.

"You, you're the reason I'm in this mess."

Kal shielded Maddie.

"You are in this mess thanks to fate. You should perhaps take this up with the man you refuse to talk with," Kal said.

Lillyanna started to storm towards him, only stopping when Eadric wrapped his arms around her.

"All I had to do was keep you away from her long enough to capture you. No. You ruined everything by bringing this guy. All I had to do was protect the labs. He'll never forgive me."

Kal really didn't care what she was going on about.

"Eadric, deal with her. I'm taking Maddie in . Let us know when we're heading to the next spot."

Ignoring the angry growls, he held tight to the only one

155

who mattered to him. The only one that would have the power to calm the dragon within him. Right now, their soul ached to touch every inch of their mate. To ensure that she was okay. To explore her body like it was a map to his dreams.

He ducked under an exposed duct in the ship and headed down the hall.

"Where are we going?" she asked, her words terse.

He liked when she had a bit of fire to kiss away.

"To bed, mate. To bed."

Crossing her arms over her chest, she smirked. At least she figured out he wasn't letting her go. Not this soon.

"Don't you dare distract me, Kal. I'm still mad about that comment. The one where you said I was more than you bargained for. What did you expect? A bunch of women all just waiting around for some dragon-alien thing to rescue them from their everyday lives?"

He thought for a moment. Yeah. That had pretty much been the point. Something in him said that wasn't the answer his Maddie would appreciate though.

"If I say no, will you stop and let me show you just how much I love you?"

16

*M*addie's heart raced as she opened her eyes to a pitch black room. No windows. Sucking in the air, her heart threatened to jump out of her chest. Where was she?

A moment later a familiar touch reached for her.

"Maddie? Are you okay?"

The warmth of his chest pressed against her "You're safe, mate. No one would dare hurt you."

Right. She was safe. She was with Kal. On a spaceship. Right. So weird. Got it. This was home for now. She waited for doubt to hit and it didn't. No. Anywhere Kal was would be home.

"Right. Sorry. Nightmare. Are we still in Roswell?"

An orange glow filled the room as Kal's tattoos lit up.

"Yes, although not for much longer. I asked that you have a chance to say goodbye to your mother."

A tear pricked her eye. Well, son of a crabapple. Mr. Muscles was sweet. She turned to him and smiled.

"You really are the man of my dreams and so much more." Maddie leaned in and kissed him.

Pulling away, her eyes adjusted to the light.

"Can we go back to the house? Or is that too dangerous?"

He studied her for a moment.

"Deo has been monitoring the area, and it looks like they are looking about twenty miles west of here. No one has gone back to the house. If you promise to be quick, we should be able to. Do you think your mother wouldn't find you here?"

She shook her head. "I honestly don't know. I just wanted to grab something from there."

Maddie ignored a burning in her arm. She'd been through so much that it was only fitting something would still hurt. Her head beat to an invisible drum of a hangover.

"Okay. Get dressed and we will set out soon. It's almost night, better to get there and back without detection."

She nodded. "How long have I been asleep?" Getting out of bed, she looked for her clothes. She needed to grab a few more clothes, and lucky for her she'd never unpacked. It felt like she'd been back in this stupid town for weeks and in reality it had only been what, a couple of days? God, if someone had told her she'd meet the man of her dreams and fall for him in a matter of days she'd never have believed them. Maddie barely believed her own eyes.

"It's been a few hours. We moved the ship, but not far enough for my comfort. We'll take one of my brothers as well. Better to have backup."

Rolling her eyes, Maddie sat on the edge of the bed. When would she ever feel like herself again?

"Kal, I love you. But, remind me. Why am I so important? Why the backup? Why don't they move the ship and then we can just come meet them."

He shrugged into his shirt.

"Maddie. We came for our mates. Our mission is you. Or well, one for each of us. If one of us can't find their mate, we will all search. The magic of our dragons is too much for our human forms to handle without our mates. Don't you feel the power?"

She sat there quietly. She had felt it so many times in the last day but she hadn't realized what it meant, really.

Closing her eyes she sat very still. Invisible tides swam through her, foreign magic exploring her. Her own magic sparked as if playing with a new friend. So crazy.

"Okay. Fine. So somehow I'm supposed to be what? An anchor? And, now that you found me. You won't what? Die?"

Maddie grabbed at her chest. Oh, was that what he'd meant? They'd die without mates? Well, hell.

He grunted in response. As if he were one with her, Kal came over and planted a kiss on her forehead.

"No, mate. I will not die. You are my everything."

Kal grabbed his jacket and Maddie couldn't help but admire his thick chest as he zipped it up. Damn, he was hot. Maybe she should thank fate, right after she said goodbye to her mom.

It was hard to breathe all of a sudden. Shit. This wasn't supposed to be the hard part. Mom had been dead for so long, yet it still seemed like yesterday.

"Ready?" Kal asked.

She nodded. Maddie couldn't trust her own voice right now.

Kal pulled her along into the hallway. Her feet struggled to move today. At least, with a little rest her head seemed more clear, and she finally noticed the ship. They walked over a solid floor, not what she'd imagined. Grates or something, cold metal. When she'd imagined a spaceship, she thought of wires and duct work too. Sure, everything was metal, it was still simple, but it didn't feel much different from some kind of contemporary design.

"This is not what I expected."

Kal smiled down at her, giving her hand a squeeze.

"What did you expect?"

Maddie shrugged. "Have you ever heard of Klingons?"

Kal let out a chest-rumbling laugh.

"They aren't real, but yes."

Oh, good. Aliens knew about pop culture, or at least hers did.

"Well, I guess that's what I thought. This is simple. The lighting is soft. I dunno, it's not scary."

She squeezed his hand back.

"Well, I guess I'm glad that you don't find us to be scary. We are protectors, not the enemy. I can't say every species out there is like us. Now, let's get your stuff and move out of the area."

Kal turned to face her as he spoke.

A shiver ran down her spine under his gaze.

"What?" she asked.

His hand rose, gently brushing a strand of loose hair behind her ear.

"Nothing. Only, sometimes everything. I just wanted to look at you, just to make sure this was all real."

His words elicited a beautiful flutter within her. Rising on her tiptoes, she kissed him.

"It's a dream, but one that you're living. Let's go, Kal. The sooner we get back, the sooner eternity starts."

Taking the lead, he led her out of the ship. She was met with a hoard of dragons.

Well, four to be exact. What it must be like back on their planet.

Kal quickly shifted, something Maddie was growing rather used to. Waiting for him to settle, she came up to the beast and ran a hand down his snout.

The eyes were still Kal, but they were also this creature. Beautiful. The Dragon sniffed her hair and blew out a breath, nudging her with his muzzle.

"Alright. Sorry. I'm still not used to you like this. Let's go, dragon boy."

Maddie slid off his back the second Kal's paws hit the ground. Her legs wobbled. Air legs, she supposed.

All she knew was what she needed, and that was to say goodbye. She was finally ready to move on. Accept her new life. Mostly.

"Mom?" she whispered as she headed for the house.

Maddie shivered, and not from the night air. Memories flooded back. It didn't matter that she knew Kal would come for her or that she would somehow make it out alive, that lab terrified her. The memories might fade, but the smells of lab and sterile environments would never fade. One foot in front of the other was all she could do to get into the house.

Her hand shook as she reached for the knob, and Maddie paused. Casting a spell to seek out energy, she waited. All life had energy although right now she probably had more than three people with her anxiety.

"It's safe. Deo already checked."

She jumped as Kal came up next to her.

"Right. Okay." Taking a hesitant step forward, she forced through the memories, the fear, the dread, and the anger.

"Mom?" she called into the space.

Nothing.

"Maybe she will find you, Maddie. Let's grab what you need. I don't like being exposed. I can't guarantee they won't be back."

Swallowing a lump in her throat, she grabbed Kal's hand and went in.

She could do this.

"Wait here? I won't be long."

Quickly, Maddie ran to the picture on the end table and grabbed it, gripping it to her chest. She needed something. Even if she never got to say a final goodbye, she'd always have a memory and echo of her past.

Clutching the picture to her chest, she walked back to the kitchen. "I just want to grab my clothes. Then we can go."

The hall suddenly tilted.

"Maddie? You okay?"

Kal's strong hands held her, keeping her from falling.

Rubbing her arm, she tried to erase the dull throb that grew with every passing beat of her heart. "I. yeah. I think so. Can we just get out of here?"

Kal nodded and pulled her to him. The room stopped spinning, and she got a few feet further. The door to her room wasn't far, she could do this. Grab her bag and walk away from this. That was it. She didn't need to wait around here.

Breathing through the unease, she tried to feel what Kal felt. Focus on figuring out a new skill. Only, it was useless against the dread rising within her. Something was wrong, but maybe it was just the memory.

A sting shot through her arm and she dropped the frame. Kal's hand shot out to grab her as she buckled. Reaching in what seemed like slow motion, the picture frame continued to fall, but Kal caught the frame as Maddie crumpled.

"Maddie? What's wrong?"

She blinked through a pain radiating through her. This was not the same thing her mother had done.

"I don't know. My arm. It's my arm."

Kal gripped her sleeve and ripped at it.

"Maddie, the doctor. At the lab. He did something before you got away, a shot of something. What was it?"

She shook her head. "I don't know. I'd forgotten about it until now."

She cried out in pain.

"Maddie? Hold on. I'm calling for help."

She had no idea what the hell was going on. A sour taste entered her mouth. Great, this was getting worse.

Healing spells. She knew some, maybe? Could she think of one though? No. Because she sucked at that. She wasn't that kind of witch. She tried to draw on strength from Kal, find the magic in the air around her.

"Maddie dear? I told you not to fight back."

Looking up, Maddie saw her mother floating.

"Oh dear. Oh dear. Why did you do this? This was the one scenario that could have gone wrong with my plan."

Another plan gone wrong. Maddie couldn't even pretend shock.

"Mom. What did you do to me?"

Her mother fidgeted. "I didn't do this. It was all going so well until you had to show that you had some of Kal's power. Oh, Maddie. Why must you always fight me?"

Kal supported her, but she couldn't sit up through the pain. Her stomach clenched, and she dry heaved.

"You tell him to get a hold of that woman, the witch that

163

Eadric will mate. She can help. Oh, if you would have just listened. That doctor poisoned you. You need to slow the spread of it down. Contact Mrs. Rivers, she will help."

Maddie blinked through watery eyes.

"My dear girl. I love you. I'm afraid this is my time to leave you. This is where I say goodbye. I can't help you anymore. I can't see your future beyond here and, finally it seems as if I've completed my remaining business."

Maddie whimpered. "But, I still need you."

Her mother's cold touch caressed her cheek.

"No. You are right where you should be. It's my time to rest. Your fate is now far away from here."

What a shitty goodbye this was. Maddie started to cry. Salty drops of anguish kissed the corner of her mouth, some tears fell on her hand, and in the end she felt a healing of her soul. She'd never cried for her mom. She'd never allowed herself to feel. Until now.

"Maddie? What happened?"

Hadn't he been there? No? Maybe he'd stepped away? She couldn't remember the last few seconds beyond her mother.

"Kal? Bring me my phone. It's somewhere here."

Standing, he looked around the room and left Maddie on the floor helpless again.

It was then she realized Kal had no idea what she was talking about.

"It's my communication to everyone, Kal. White and rectangle, about the size of my hand. I know it's here. I didn't have it with me when those stupid Illuminati assholes grabbed me.

"Right. The small rectangle." After a second he took several purposeful steps into the other room.

"Here? Is this it? It was behind the door." He held it out for her. "How do you use it?"

Maddie held up her hand. "Push the buttons." She winced in pain.

Jabbing at the screen, she waited for it to wake up. Less than two percent of her battery. Great.

"Who are you communicating with?"

Squinting, Maddie tried to see through the blur in her vision.

"My mother, did you hear her? She said to slow the poison, we needed to call someone. Wait, did you get through to Eadric or someone?"

Kal nodded. "Yes, I did. And no, I didn't see your mother. Was she here?"

Shaking her head, maybe she was hallucinating.

"I. I don't know. She did say that we need that witch. The one Eadric kidnapped. Maybe I'm hallucinating that I saw my mother. I don't even know."

Kal scooped her up.

"Fine. Just push the buttons to the woman you need. Eadric is trying to control his witch. She doesn't want to cooperate." We're to meet them back at the ship."

She was too tired to argue.

"Fine. But wait until I reach my mother's friend."

Finally, she found the contact in her phone. A million years passed with each ring. Her arm threatened to collapse as the phone grew heavy.

Worst fucking trip home ever.

As her muscles gave, she reached over and hit speaker right as the incessant ringing stopped.

"Maddie, dear? Is that you?"

Not how she'd expected to be greeted. She hadn't seen

Mrs. Rivers since the funeral. Channeling strength from Kal, she finally got her voice working again.

"Yes. Mrs. Rivers. It's me. You. My mother." Well, hell. This wasn't going well. "Can you help?"

There was a pause. "So it happened? Your mother had warned me you might have a run in with the local quacks. I'll be right over."

"These women in your town. They are strange," said Kal, as he pulled her closer. She didn't think that there was any more space between them, but she was wrong.

"Yeah. Welcome to my world. Couch. Can you put me on the couch?"

Thankfully, she didn't need to ask twice.

"Also, can you go put a towel on or something?"

Naked Kal was something she enjoyed, and maybe something his shifter brothers seemed resigned to. Human women, probably not.

"She's old, Kal."

He looked down and shook his head. After he made sure Maddie wasn't going anywhere, that she seemed safe, he walked off muttering to himself.

"You can give her a heart attack -" Maddie worked to get more air. "After she saves my life."

Crap, she was already out of breath. After today, Maddie would be better about not getting kidnapped. This was all her mother's damn fault. But, really it wasn't. It was fate's fault. Maddie wanted to hate fate, but then she would never have met Kal. She'd never have let him in.

Maddie awoke to voices. Her eyes skittered around the room. Right. Okay. Her mom's house. When had she fallen asleep?

"Oh wonderful, Maddie dear. I need you to drink this."

Mrs. Rivers' short and squat frame toddled over. Maddie shielded her eyes as her lemon yellow hair came into view.

"I. Your hair?"

Mrs. Rivers smiled. "Yes dear. The purple had to go. Now drink this up. One big gulp. Don't ask what's in it. Just swallow."

Maddie took a flask with the cap already removed. She then made the mistake of smelling it. If her stomach hadn't been churning before it was now.

"Always fighting instruction, Madison. Well, just know it only tastes half as bad."

Not really helping.

Maddie, do it. Please.

Kal knelt next to her. "The woman says it will slow your system down, suspend the poison."

She turned to him, looking deep into the orange that had intrigued her from the very first moment she'd seen him.

The color was wrong though. Almost murky.

"Kal?"

He shook his head.

Don't expel any more energy. Drink.

Without looking away, she felt the rippling of magic where his hand slid beneath her own. He lifted her hand, bringing the flask to her lips.

With a single nod of his head she did as told.

Oh, God! That tasted worse.

She started to gag. Nope, this wasn't going down. Shit.

"Wait. Wait a moment. Just swallow, dear. Don't fight the potion."

Mrs. Rivers' soft wrinkled hand settled on her brow and a calming void started to set in. She felt her hand begin to slip down; the flask falling.

"Sleep, dear one. Your warrior will fix this. Go, warrior. Time is your enemy now more than those scientists."

Those were the last words she heard before she fell into a black emptiness. The only comfort around her was the swirl of Kal's magic, his dragon coming in and out of the void of her mind.

He would save her.

EPILOGUE

"*M*addie? Maddie? Wake up."

Kal's deep baritone filtered through the haze in her head.

"Is it working?"

Maddie didn't know that voice.

"I don't know. I can feel her though. Stirring. Something is happening. It has to work."

A chair dragged against the floor. Someone coughed. Hushed voices came from all directions.

The fog started to clear. Maddie could see the end of a long tunnel, and on the other side was Kal. She'd follow him wherever he went.

"Is it working?"

Kal grunted, Maddie was sure of that voice.

"Eadric, ask one more time and I'm going to lose my shit."

There was a pause.

"Dude. I'm just asking. You have no idea what it took to get that shit. I have bruises on top of bruises."

Maddie laughed at the banter.

"Her chest moved. Did you see that?"

A hand rested on top of her sternum. That had better be Kal. God, why was it taking so long to get out of her own mind. Maddie remembered what had happened. Poison, Mrs. Rivers making her drink sewage, Kal's dragon keeping her company. So this had to be a good sign. They must have tracked down the cure. Wonderful. So why the hell wasn't she waking up.

"She's been breathing, Eadric. We didn't kill her, she was just in a deep sleep."

More shuffling. Maddie's mind kept running. Literally. Was there an end to this tunnel? For crap sake, if this would burn calories maybe she wouldn't mind so much. Right now though, damn it. How does one escape their own mind?

"Can someone fetch that old witch? Maybe something's wrong?" Kal asked.

Someone touched her arm.

"The blue lines are gone. The antidote worked. I don't know why she isn't waking up."

Well this was a kicker. How in the hell did she get an antidote to work and yet still couldn't wake up. One eyelid. That's all she had to move. Come on. It's a tiny muscle. Nothing.

"Did someone find the communication device, the phone? The woman is on there."

A female voice she'd never heard answered Kal.

"Is it the last one she called? Do you know her passcode? Oh wait, it's a thumb print. Hold up her finger."

Maddie wanted to yank her damn hand away from some woman looking at her phone. What the heck. That woman better be far away from her Kal.

"It was the last person communicated with. Yes. Rivers," Kal said.

The electric charge of Kal's touch against her hand - the only thing keeping her sane right now. She would figure this out. She had to. She was smart.

"Got it. The phone's ringing."

The room got so quiet that Maddie couldn't even hear breathing. Wow. Serious much? She was fine. She was just stuck. Mrs. Rivers probably did something dumb. She was a bit of a meddlesome witch, probably why her mother had gotten along with her so well.

"Hello?"

A pause.

"Yes. No."

Another pause

"No, she won't wake up."

Kal's hand left hers. The tension rolled off him. God, Maddie wanted to make him feel better. She just couldn't figure out how.

"Kal? You won't believe this," said the female again.

Who was this woman? Maddie was not a fan of this mystery.

"The woman said it's a Sleeping Beauty potion."

Silence again. Seriously, this silence thing did her no good when she couldn't escape her head.

"Are we supposed to know what that means?" said another male voice Maddie couldn't place.

"You're kidding. None of you know what or who Sleeping Beauty is?"

A lot of grumbles. Apparently all the brothers were there. Wonderful. She probably looked like death. Well, Kal loved her and that was all that mattered. Right?

"Oh for crap's sake. Kiss her."

Another chair scratched the floor. If they ruined these

wood floors, well, well she wouldn't be here to care about it. But still.

"Kiss her?" asked Kal.

Maddie wanted to smile. When had Kal ever not taken the opportunity to kiss her. This should be easy.

"Yes. Kiss her. It's like the fairy tale. Princess falls into a deep sleep and the only way to wake her up is by true love's kiss. Being that you idiots seriously believe in fate and all that, this is right up your alley. So just kiss her."

Maddie might actually like this woman, she thought. The couch suddenly shifted.

Here it comes. The final piece to the puzzle. She should have known Mrs. Rivers would use some kind of dumb spell like this.

It felt like the first kiss all over again. Maddie would have held her breath if she could control anything except the endless abyss of her thoughts.

The warmth of his breath tingled against her cold lips. He tasted of desire and a salty sweet she hungered for as he claimed her mouth.

The sensation of everything around her. The cold in her body, the warmth of his, the ache of her bruised arm. Everything flooded in.

She parted her lips, letting him in.

Okay then. Maybe we should return to the ship," said someone.

Another cleared their throat. "Kal. Um. It, uh, seems to be working. So just report…"

Maddie giggled and pushed him back.

"Hey."

Opening her eyes, the bright light of day hurt. The eclipse of Kal's face was all she needed to focus on as she squinted.

His orange-gold eyes the only thing she ever wanted to see for the rest of her life.

"Hey," he replied.

"Thanks for saving me."

He nodded. "I didn't do much. Eadric has a story to tell once you're better."

She smiled. "The only story I want to know is, when do we leave?"

COMING SOON

Space Dragons Seek Mates
Book 1: Must Love Dragons

Coming 2020!
Book 2: Single Red Dragon
Eadric would do anything for the woman he loves, except
sacrifice his bother's happiness.

Book 3: Dragon Wanted
Book 4: Looking for a Good Dragon
Book 5: No Scales Needed
Book 6: Desperately Seeking Dragon

ABOUT THE AUTHOR

Michelle's imagination started spilling out onto paper the second she could scribble. Her drawing never improved, but her love affair with words continued and evolved as she became infatuated with one story after another. If life could be written, Michelle would write everyone's ending as a happily ever after.

Michelle grew up in Chicago and later moved to Colorado. Her husband still makes fun of her Midwest accent. She has traded in her engineering degree to raise two little humans and three dogs, and prays she survives it all. Her sanity survives on the pages she writes. As Michelle always says, in a world of serious she writes an escape.

Website: http://www.michellezieglerauthor.com
Newsletter: http://michellezieglerauthor.com/contact/

facebook.com/MichelleZieglerAuthor
twitter.com/MZiegler_Writer
instagram.com/mziegler_writer

Made in United States
Orlando, FL
09 December 2023